# LONDON KENI ENGLAND:
## Heavenly Dreams

### A NOVEL

## Deeann England

iUniverse, Inc.
New York   Bloomington

London Keni England: Heavenly Dreams
A Novel

This is a work of fiction. All of the characters, names, incidents,
organizations, and dialogue in this novel are either the products
of the author's imagination or are used fictitiously.

iUniverse books may be ordered through booksellers or by contacting:

iUniverse
1663 Liberty Drive
Bloomington, IN 47403
www.iuniverse.com
1-800-Authors (1-800-288-4677)

ISBN: 978-1-4401-7279-3 (pbk)
ISBN: 978-1-4401-7277-9 (cloth)
ISBN: 978-1-4401-7278-6 (ebk)

Printed in the United States of America

iUniverse rev. date: 9/3/2009

For my sister, London, the best sister in the world. Peace.

# Contents

# Chapter 1
# Ascender

## London Keni England

"LONDON ENGLAND?...LONDON ENGLAND?" she heard her name again only clearer "LONDON ENGLAND?...LONDON ENGLAND?" Why did she feel so strange and weightless? Was she dreaming? Was it a heat stroke? Was this a coma? She had been her only brother's pal on rainy days so she was tough as nails and fainting wasn't like her so why get an airy feeling now? There it was again. "Paging London England, London England?" Who was calling her and why did she find it so hard to reply? Maybe she remembered her only sister teaching her that being tough was good, but it's also necessary to be wise and cautious. Her own way of dealing with situations was to maintain an approach of wait and see, usually letting someone else more aggressive take charge. Maybe she was hoping that it would just stop. No such luck. "London England, London England, Respond London England?" Now she thought 'this is too much.' She had always liked her name. She had kind, sensitive parents who had saved their witty title for the youngest of three children. They had even gone so far as making the baby's middle name unique by changing the father's name, Kenneth, to a feminine Keni. And so was born London Keni

England. But at this particular moment in time, for the first time since kindergarten children sang, "London's britches are falling down," did she feel her name sounded odd or foreign. With desperate attempts to gain her own awareness of where she was and why, she followed the decent laws of nature and etiquette and answered, "Yes?" INSTANT FLASH, SONIC WHITE and then she could see all around her. The colors were glorious. What she saw was sparkling, brilliant and wonderful. If there was a better adjective for tranquility, then it would be that too. Like diamonds and pearls combined. This seemed to be true perfection and happiness. Reality was only relevant and she needed answers fast. Her mind was thinking of what to do next, selecting through survival logic that had been passed down by her mother, Nita. Her body was calm and her eyes were free to absorb all the new scenery before her. She saw figures that seemed to be slide-gliding at land level, up close and in the distance. But her immediate attention was starting at the top with lime green clouds and an all white carpet. It appeared that Dr. Seuss and Walt Disney had collaborated on every inch of this place. As London was wondering about the crystal streamers that appeared to come from a million miles overhead, she heard the voice again. This time the name was very asian. "Tri Truigh...Tri Truigh?... Tri Truigh Tri Truigh...Please respond Tri Truigh , Tri Truigh..." as the voice faded..."Where am I?" asked a delicate voice almost right beside London. Startled from her own exploration, London tried to speak, but Tri came back at her in a quick and impatient string of questions, "Wha happe to me? Who is calling my name? What last thing you 'member? I ememba noffing. Who otha white people? This some big Hollywood show? Or, not-so-funny joke? My fatha, he the GI JOE, my motha full Asian. This some big fat American conspiracy? You talk to my fatha. He tells you…" London wasn't listening anymore to Tri because she had already spit out the most important question of all; where were our families?

London wasn't listening to the names being called or the muffled confusion that followed, she was in her own personal panic and trying desperately to put things into perspective. She started by thinking about her immediate family and then her own unit, husband, Jim Madrid and her beautiful step daughter Brandi. How London missed them right now. She was trying to stay focused and think of nothing but thoughts of them and their home in Texas. London began to concentrate on their house. It was a lovely ranch in Alice, Texas. It was close enough to Corpus Christi that they could still get to the beach within an hours time. Not only did they get their long awaited property but they had found enough land that London could have all of her dog training classes. She kept kittens, rabbits and horses also, but her Great Dane's, Lobo and Moose, were the 'top dogs' of the entire ranch. Jim had worked for many years at FedEx to save enough for London's business. It seemed like an odd choice at first but her business "PET-I-CURES" had taken off quicker than anyone had imagined. She loved being able to do matching manicures for master and pets. Further, a lot of the Texas women were very wealthy, fashionable and generous. Her own products 'Pet Polish and Claw Colors' were now everywhere. This, in return, allowed Jim to finally follow his dream of being a chef. It had only been two years since he parked his semi for the last time and bought his restaurant. And yet, they were already in a home that they owned and living life on their own terms... But where was he now? What happened to...

"Welcome Returners. By now your alert levels should be rising. We welcome you to Upper Anaheim. Please stand by for your orientation and instructions." Upper Anaheim? London recognized Anaheim because she had spent her entire life telling people that Anaheim is where she was born but had left when she was only months old. But, Upper-Anaheim? She had never heard of this place and how did she get to California, anyway? She had always heard it was crazy out here but this place was way beyond any metro-plex that she had ever seen. Had she won a trip and was so excited that she didn't come to until now? But she would have brought Jim and Brandi. They had always found time on the weekends to be with the Brandi and do special things. There is no way that London could have left them behind. She struggled again to remember the last thing she could before hearing her own name. She and Brandi had been playing with the iguanas, Igon and Iggy, while Jim had barbequed. Yes, she could recall that. They had eaten fajitas out back on the deck. Jim had cleaned the dishes and had come back outside with shampoo for the dogs because they were both sporting leftovers like a beard. They had all three helped in the dog washing and then Brandi had excused herself to take her hour long shower. London smiled to herself. At least part of the child was all girl. She might be able to beat the boys her age at everything she tried, but when it came to primping, she was unstoppable. London thought back further, to all the pretend beauty, cheerleading and karaoke contests in which she was her sole announcer, audience and judge. Brandi had enough imagination to live three days in one. All those summers spent together while Jim was at work had made them the best of friends. It was only recently that Jim had been able to be home during the day and witness Brandi's shows with full appreciation. Brandi and London had practiced all day so after the barbeque and after the dog bath and finally after her shower, the coffee table was moved and London began with a clear, loud tone: "Ladies and gentlemen, The Solace Ranch is proud to present Brandi Madrid." Brandi had chosen some of her own songs and had insisted on playing them each three times, just to make sure the listeners got the full affect...And maybe to stretch her bedtime just a little. After the third time she was finally pleased with her outcome so with one last gulp of juice she was off to her room leaving London and Jim laughing hysterically. Yes, it had been a nice day and a lovely evening. London was positive that there had been no mention of a day trip or a vacation. Maybe she was home and in bed and still dreaming. This was just the most powerful and real-like dream that she had ever experienced. Just when London was feeling better she was interrupted by another voice.

"Attention Returners, we apologize for the delay, we were gathering all of your past information and preparing it for disintegration. That being done, we are now ready to move forward. As most of you have figured out by now, you are no longer a citizen of the planet Earth. We phrase it as molecular relocation. Your soul, or orb, will remain with you through all three phases of enlightenment. It is only your temple or your container that will adjust to its astronomy needs. The first stage on Earth you are new, solid and strong. The second stage, HERE, is to become older, wiser and lighter, commonly known as the Utopia Stage. This bliss growing, period will last five years of our calendar and then you will move on to the third and final stage, total enlightenment and pure energy form. We know this is a lot for you to grasp in such a few moments, but soon your host will be beside you and you will be able to ask your personalized questions...Thank you for your attention and again, welcome."

So there it was the horrible truth. This was no dream. It wasn't one of Jim Madrid's special surprises. The voice said that she was dead. NO! Something inside of her said this was all wrong. Not her, not now, not when everything on earth was already heaven to her. What would her mom say? Who would take care of Brandi? How long would she have to wait to see her Jim Madrid again? She suddenly felt so sad that she hadn't changed her last name to his. They had always agreed that she should keep her name London England. But now she longed to be even more connected to him that just a hyphen England-Madrid. How may people had commented and laughed about their unusual coincidence? And now she couldn't even grin at hearing someone very close to her almost whispering..."London....London England?... Are you London England?"

The Greeter had such a melodic tone that London didn't hesitate to turn to her right and answer, "Yes."

"Hi, I'm Lydia and I am here to help you. I am sorry about the wait. Usually we have a full description of each Returner, but some of your information was scrambled in the telelift and I wasn't sure if you were male or female." She continued, "Most of the others have already left the telestation. Shall we begin our journey now? We can talk on the way to your Interview Inn."

London jumped in, "I'm sorry, my what?"

"Your Interview Inn, your resting place," said Lydia.

With a gasp and stopping in her tracks, London said, "My resting place...Already?"

Slightly laughing, Lydia apologized, "I am very sorry. I forget that on Earth we used to call a grave a resting place. Please forgive me. I think a long time ago it was called 'An Entrance Interview Inn Institute,' but it has been shortened to 'Interview Inn,' or AEIII. It is where you receive your directions. We find the adjustment from Earth to the Utopia Stage is very difficult, so we greet you upon returning which gives us the opportunity to explain what is going to happen and then we take you to the AEIII to meet your Placer, and THERE is where you get your directions."

"How to do what?" an unaware London asked her Greeter.

"Not what, where! Directions for where you will go after this," said Lydia.

"Oh, you can't tell me? Do you know anything? What's going to happen there?" urged London.

Again Lydia giggled, "No, I am more like an assistant. I chose to stay here as a Transition Hostess instead of receiving directions. They said my zing was unreadable." She shrugged a confused tress not knowing that zing just meant energy. "It's glorious fun to help Returners here. I feel fuller with every encounter."

# CHAPTER 2
# Upper Anaheim

## LONDON AND LYDIA

London proceeded with confused caution, "Unreadable? Why do you call us Returners? Have I been alive before? And, at what place are you talking about?"

This time it was Lydia who stopped walking and smiled. "If you are thinking of reincarnation it is not like that. It is one soul, one life cycle of three stages. The reason why we say returning is because this is where you were born. Everyone goes back to the place of their birth, so they can be telelifted to the next level. Our hearts never forget where it woke up the first time so it has to return full circle to get good closure of the energy orb."

London asked slowly, "Is there a hell, is it people who don't get back or didn't fill their orb with the right energy?"

"Nope, that is an Earth myth...A scare tactic. Each soul has a true passion and path. We are all energy, collecting energy, no pain, and no fire. I suppose some could have less."

London couldn't help whisper, "I am in pain now. I miss Jim, Brandi and my pets. I want to go back."

"You do? How odd. You are not supposed to carry the selfless thoughts and love feelings with you. You should be gearing up for selfish adventures," Lydia explained.

London tried not to cry. "But, I do miss them and I do still want to take care of and be with them. I am too young to die, I am only thirty seven. Who ever heard of a thirty-seven year old dying in their sleep? That's not natural causes and what about my information being scrambled? Something is wrong, I can sense it. You said yourself Lydia that you didn't even know if I was a male or female."

"Yes, that is true, but your Placer will have more knowledge about these things to help you with your directions. I am here to make sure you are comfortable and delivered to be processed. I regret that I don't have more data or control over your case."

London could tell that Lydia really had no other facts, so she eased off. "Well, what is this different place that you keep mentioning?"

Lydia smiled again, "Not place, places, and a Placer...here there are several different heavens, one for each of the suns. Your Placer will either analyze which sector you should be in, or like me, you can choose to stay here and become a Greeter. It is for the same span as enlightenment. If you leave, it is your joy that fills your orb. If you stay, it is the joy of helping others that will make your soul-cell full."

All London could say was "Oh," and then a very slow "Wow." She thought that she should ask more questions but at the moment she found herself wondering about Lydia. She too, looked too young to be here. Maybe she was even younger than London. She had long, dark, thick hair that made London's mind jump to Brandi's own gorgeous mane. But unlike Brandi's dark brown eyes, Lydia had gold-green eyes to show her mixed heritage. Electric eyes that were as light green as the streaks that London got in her blonde strands after swimming all summer.

Sensing that London was staring at her, Lydia asked, "What is it? Is there something else you wanted to know about? No, we don't have any other color of cover but white. White robes for Returners, white robes for Greeters and white robes for Placers."

Happy for the humor and the open spot, London chuckled, paused and said as politely as possible, "What about you? Why are you here? I mean, I know why you are still here, or rather, why you haven't moved on. But I was wondering why you are here at all. How did you die?"

"Oh that," an unemotional Lydia replied, "Remember when I said we were all energy?" Without waiting for London to answer she continued, "I think that sometimes when we are making our journey to Earth for the first time that some accidents occur to a random few. Maybe hit by a comet, scorched by the sun or acid rain. Things like that. Me? They called it Leukemia. I think that when we, or rather, by the time we get to our final destination that we are cleansed enough to join the energy ring. I hear it is nothing but goodness of the Universe and eventually every being ends up there. Lore is only told in small portions on this telestation, but it is told that in your last galaxy planet post, the truth will be revealed. Similar to Earth, we are on a need to know basis." Lydia shrugged, "Does that make sense? Thank you for asking about me. I hope that makes things a little clearer or easier to take?"

With that, and without answering, London continued walking in silence beside Lydia. London could sense their trek was almost up. It had been a pleasant walk. The footpaths were like pure white cotton and they had led through something resembling a town square with lovely pink and orange tree masses. There were no streets and no cars and the few tall buildings in the background looked fragile and lacy as if woven from white plastic. Tiny purple pansy-looking flowers covered the ground and the air was as sweet as Esperanza plants in the spring. Lydia began tour guiding saying the structures were all telestations that were placed directly over the hospitals on earth to make going and coming more convenient, and that the smaller silver buildings that sparkled on the outskirts were their quarters. And lastly, just as Lydia started to describe the testing, they came upon a beautiful structure labeled the 'Interview Inn March Plaza.' Here, at last, was their destination and London would now be meeting her Placer.

Although the area seemed empty and deserted, Lydia assured

London that her Placer would still be here and that she would return (no pun intended) quickly. With that she began climbing the see-through stairs which numbered more than twenty and led up to the door of the Interview Inn. Moments later London saw Lydia reappear at the top of the stairs. She wasn't alone. She was accompanied by a very pleasant looking man who, like Lydia, wore a simple white toga. Only it was longer and had a wide silver belt. London imagined that it was probably the male version of the 'appropriate' dress and thought he looked like the nicest person that she had ever met. He spoke with Lydia as they ascended towards London. London assumed that Lydia's next assignment was being mapped out for her.

"That didn't take long. Did it?" Lydia asked as they approached London. Without waiting for an answer Lydia finished with, "London, I would like you to meet your Placer, Robbie. I have to leave you now, but trust truth that you will be in excellent hands."

Robbie chimed in so sweetly and quickly that she hardly noticed the disappearance of Lydia. "Well hello London. Your Greeter, Lydia, has told me a little bit about your case. I am sorry about the scrambled journey. I will try to have an explanation for you before you depart. Please don't feel worry. Just know that everything has its perfect form and perfect time so we are here to help you and make this a lovely pre-experience for you. You can call me Robbie or you can call me Bob. I feel both are fine Earth names. My full title is Robert of Upper-Anaheim, but I started having my guests use nicknames back when I was a Greeter and now it has just kind of stuck. My time here has gone very quickly and it has been very enjoyable and most importantly fulfilling. Oh sure, sometimes I wonder what is happening on the Heaven Planets, or how the Returners are doing that I have placed along the way. But at least this way I get to meet each kind of personality and stay up on all the different destinations. Oh, wow, I have been rambling. Let's go inside, I will answer any questions you might have and then we will get started."

They climbed the stairs together. It was London who spoke first. "Where is everyone?"

Robbie explained, "Our areas are like any other travel stations, there are very busy times and then there are down times after everyone has been processed." He continued, "For instance, today, in your case, you arrived with about 50 other Returners all of which were very cut and dry. No duo personalities. And quite frankly, you are the first case of gender question that I have ever seen. As I said, my goal here is to make your future better. Do you know what your passion is?" London stuttered a silent yes but Robbie kept going. "Well, dismiss your definition that is associated with intimacy. What we deal with here is the TRUE SELF passion. Since you have already been cleansed of your material world layers, we are able to hone in on the kind of passion and dedication that are hidden at the center of all humans."

London broke in, "But I do have passion like that…For my husband, Jim, and my daughter, Brandi, and my animals and my life in Texas."

"Highly irregular!" exclaimed Robbie. His voice was louder and fuller than London had heard it be so far. 'There' she thought maybe she was finally getting someone's attention. "OK, Lydia did indicate that there were signs of nonreturning, but we must take this one step at a time," began a quieter Robbie. "You say you have a clear, vivid memory of your em, er, well, uh, past life? And you say that you still feel your heart tugging inside you? Does it feel pulled down in your stomach, like your heart is causing you illness? Or is it tugging you up to your smile like an anxious grin shiver?"

London cried out immediately, "Down, way down …Down like homesick. I want to go back. I have more to do and more to see. I want to see Beenie grow up. I want to train my first batch of Great Dane puppies. I still have to pay off my mom…And spend more time with Jim now that we are able. We haven't even been to London England yet and we always promised each other we would, then Spain…" stammering, she tried so hard to go on and blurt out all the convincing arguments why she should get to go back to Earth. But Robbie interrupted without meaning to…

"Interesting, I have heard of these isolated cases, but as long as I have been here I have never seen such grieving. Our goal is fulfillment, not sadness. We must continue with your testing now, but I promise I will look into your scrambled data. Ok? We have an error proof way of determining which Heaven Planet that you are supposed to attend. Maybe in the process of the analysis we can also answer why your Earth emotions have remained with you. Sound fair?"

London couldn't help but like him and couldn't help herself from agreeing. Logically, her first question, "So what do I have to do?"

Robbie, still continuing with his orientation said, "The way that we rate your soul is through five simple tests. There is no pain, no influence and no one to answer to in the end. At this moment, you can trust truth that the universe is yours."

Even more confused now London's blank stare said it all, but she couldn't help but prove that she was not grasping the concept by adding, "OK, whatever, so If I pass this can I go back and make breakfast with Beenie?"

Robbie replied honestly and flatly, "London, I promised you that I would research your data, which I will. But also know that I have never witnessed or heard of any Upper-errors and I have never heard of anyone going to Earth from here. This phase, after all, is for positive rejuvenation as preparation for your purest energy form. You can trust truth that our life cycle flow system is as predictable as our suns." Touching her arm he added quieter, "And my tests are not about reversal, they are only about forward motion and moving on…I am a Placer, and I become that goal, to analyze which Heaven Planet would give you optimum fuel for your soul-orb cells." Less serious, he chuckled, "I am starting to sound like a Knowledge Collector, let's move on to the fun stuff, I always start with the basics. There are three things that are constant no matter where you are placed because they all have to do with the regaining of energy…Food, sleep and love. Food in a smaller way now still provides sustenance for the soul and has happiness and/ or celebrating quality to it. Sleep is a time to store up pure energy and to help keep our citizens on some kind of familiar continuity until the third stage. Without schedules humans tend to get run down and out of sorts because they are never sure what they should be doing or when it is time for relaxing. Spending all of your time 'free' and guessing tends to be taxing on the soul after awhile instead of rejuvenating. Your purpose of passion tends to call or tug at your soul causing confusion instead of peace…And lastly, love. Love for where you get to be, love for what you get to do, and love for the like-souls who are around you. These three things to remember will help to strengthen the inner you."

London was glad that she had heard the entire presentation before the doors were opened because she was so taken aback by the beauty that awaited her that she heard nothing that Robbie had said for moments.

The tall white walls had glass panels sewn in between each section. And although it was very clinical it was also very inviting, like the atmosphere of a school for brainiac kids. High in the sunlit atrium tops were geometric shapes that were mirrored on one side and powder pastel colors on the other. There seemed to be a 10 degree drop in the temperature and huge, white, double doors leading into five different rooms. Towards the rear of the building, the water in the fountain was blue, but the plants around the bottom were not green... they were pink and magenta with dark, purple monkey grass as its base. London was curious about the plants and curious about the empty desk at the opposite side of the room. "Has your assistant gone with the others?"

Now it was Robbie that looked puzzled with her, "I don't have an assistant, why do you ask?"

London explained while pointing to the empty desk "No one is here to check about my data."

With one understanding nod Robbie said, "Oh, I see, no, well, believe it or not, this whole building is my Placer Station, I am the boss and the 'gopher'. Each of these doorways lead to testing tubes, but they are all for my use only. The desk that you see is mine. I have no need for an office but I do have personal quarters. Not many people ask about such little details. Usually they are very eager to get on to their destination but since you asked, I could show you...Would you like to see my 'resting place'? Are you interested in staying on as a Greeter?"

"No, I am interested in staying on Earth," London said with more attitude than she had intended.

"By definition, you can not 'stay' where you no longer are, and it doesn't sound like you want to help others get to where they need to be so we will carry on as planned with your chosen course," He said all of this quickly as he started off across the room and then as an afterthought added, "Don't you want to fill up your soul-orb? Everybody does."

"But I haven't chosen any course!" Yelling after him London once again couldn't help but follow.

He began slide-gliding away from the desk. The front door on his left, and the huge white doors on the right, instead, headed straight towards the waterfall. When they reached it, Robbie made a sharp left and following the dark purple monkey grass around the back to yet another huge, white door. Once inside, London was surprised again. Light tan linen was a noticeable constant with dark brown accents. There was a modest sleeping quarters in foam green and a spotless kitchenette. When she said spotless, that is exactly what she meant. No stove, no sink and no mess. There was one drawer, one cupboard and one enormous freezer.

Robbie began, "We have icefood, creamfood and a little bit of fruit, which do you prefer?" London stuttered but she never really answered because Robbie went on. "You see, here we have perfect light, so perfect heat, so perfect weather and not a big need for nourishment through food. We don't travel to the other planets so we have our food supply simplified to everyone's favorite: Cool, light and delicious. I have both icefood, which is like popsicles, snowcones and slushies. And creamfood, which is like dreamsicles, pushups or yogurt." London picked the latter, then followed him back out to his desk. Robbie told her to enjoy her creamfood and wait for him there while he made good on his promise to check with a Senior Placer who had the April-Plaza. London just knowing that the mistake would be sorted out, felt better at that moment than since the whole ordeal began. After all, she hadn't ever given up before, and she was not about to start now. She would take their test; she would do what they instructed and then show them that she was not supposed to die yet. The Senior Placer, he would know what to do and soon she would be back on her ranch in Texas.

As she finished her cool snack Robbie appeared at the doorway, told her that someone was looking into what should and/or could be done concerning her case and as he had suspected, they were supposed to move on with the 'discovery quiz'. He explained further that the tests were actually more enjoyable then they sounded. It would consist of five modules, that took very little time and that they were designed for each growth stage. They were called: Visionostic, Consciouskey, Hearticheck, the Mindopsy and everyone's favorite, the Soulotomy. After his mini-presentation, Robbie gave London a cute little wink and with that he disappeared into door number one.

Robbie took a few moments behind the closed door of room number one, and now stood at it's opening while summoning for London to join him. She rose from the desk and headed towards him, wishing that she could duck behind the waterfall and hide instead of taking this mandatory torture-quiz. As if reading her mind, Robbie began in an easy manner..."London, I do not want you to feel worry about this at all. You can trust truth that I would not let anything or anyone harm you. Most of our transits say that they love the whole process. We start out very simple. The first module is the Visionostic. It isn't like the eye chart of Earth, it is to measure your true vision of yourself and soul, OK?"

"Ok. How do we do that?" asked London.

"Simple, come inside and I will show you." With that, Robbie opened the door wide enough to let London squeeze through.

# CHAPTER 3
## Interview Inn

### LONDON AND ROBBIE

As she began to lead the way for them both, she was awestruck by the room that was surrounding her. The only color was SILVER. It looked like they could have been at the North Pole. The beautiful, oval, silver settee that was in the middle of the room was not only huge, but the main focal point and the only piece of furniture that she recognized. The implement stems that hovered all around it looked like silver corn stalks with fuzzy silver tassels…Pinkish-silver pebbles were bursting out of the top. The walls were covered in chrome that was outlined along the ceiling with silver-neon lights. The only other designated area in the entire vast room was an observation station for Robbie. A silver stool in the shape of an S was paired with a waffle type screen in the corner. As Robbie helped London onto the couch, he began to speak, "Ms. England, This may look like an ordinary chair but the truth is, it is very special. Its curve is molded for optimum comfort. The silver, we found through testing, is the best color for reflecting the Visionostic signals and the added speck guards assists us in making sure that we get the right results every time. We NEED to get you relaxed so that we can get an accurate reading, so I am going to recline the settee and turn on the soulstacks to keep all the negative sound and vibrations away from you, OK? We only want what's coming from inside you, not the environment."

London couldn't answer but rather shook her head. Her attention was on the small silver bubbles that were beginning to collect around her body and face. There were enormous silver feather dusters that were beginning to lower over her head. She was trying to touch the small silver bubbles but they seemed to stay 2 inches away from her hands at all times. Wherever she reached they would float up, or out or away.

She leaned back and began to enjoy the atmosphere while Robbie was nodding and speaking her directions, "That's the idea London. It's best if you relax your body, muscles, mind and heart. Erase any mechanical thoughts from your mind right now and concentrate on the feather duster that is erasing your worries. Visualize the soft, slow, cleansing sweeps of the soulstacks." As hard as she tried, London could not void her brain right now. This was all too new and too exciting. And this machine didn't make her feel like she was sleeping or relaxing. It seemed to be retro and thrilling to her. So much so that before she realized what she was doing she heard herself giggling out loud. She waited for Robbie to correct her or change the test but he didn't. He let her be herself, which made her laugh ever more and then by giggling she noticed that the silver bubbles around her were starting to hum, which made her chuckle even harder and when she did that they began to GLOW! Now glowing, humming, and floating bubbles??? That got her attention. She looked over towards Robbie for some insight. At first he was whistling and dancing in sweet bouncing movements to the humming, but then began to slow the dusters down and turn the lights back up.

London spoke..."I am sorry. Did I fail? Did I break it? I tried to concentrate, I really did. It is just so much fun...Just like you said."

Calmly, Robbie answered, "You were perfect. There is no right or wrong. We were not testing your self control. We were testing your content, or your personality. The characteristics the room number one deals with is eager verses content, if you are a go-getter or a wait-and-see. With this machine, it is revealed by a HI or LOW glow, if you have an active soul or a quiet soul. And believe it or not, one of the most accurate ways to see is this test. Your giggling was a sign of positive energy. If you were a negative...You would have fallen asleep. Either way is correct. This isn't about right or wrong. It's about you...and the truth. And so concludes our first test."

London was surprised and sorry to leave the room. It turned out to be so much fun that she could have let them tickle her for two more hours. This admission of joy made her remember her childhood and how, even then, she loved to be tickled. Lost in her own thoughts, she had to pull herself out because Robbie was pressing on and he was already headed toward the door to exit.

London asked quietly, "Will the other tests be as nice as this one?"

"Yes, they are." And without the need for more, he volunteered, "I think you will enjoy each one in a different way...Returners say it is a very fulfilling process the whole way through, which is wonderful to hear because that, again, is our main goal...To fill your soul with joy. But the best is yet to come, because compared to your Heaven Planet; this is nothing...Just the preliminaries. Shall we continue?"

"Please" was London's one word answer.

Robbie began describing the next analysis as they entered door number two. London expected this room to be like the last but it wasn't. This room was nothing like the rest of the building. The colors of the walls were midnight blue, almost black. There was nothing, absolutely nothing, in the room except for one chair. London shrugged her shoulders and headed for it with mild complaints. "This doesn't look like fun. I can't believe it is so dark in here."

Robbie stopped her before she could sit down." The chair is for me, and things are not always as they appear. Most humans find this highly enjoyable." As he sat in the blue woven chair, there was a swing being lowered from the ceiling. Not a regular swing. This one had a foot base of five feet wide, like the bottom of an old fashioned sewing machine.

It was not solid, but more of a grated affect that resembled lace. About 4 feet from the base was a bar that went from one side to the other for a handrail. Robbie motioned for London to climb aboard.

He was pleased to see that she was smiling. He began his introductions: "We call this one Consciouskey. The only thing that you have to do is take a ride and have a brief conversation with me. We get the best results if you don't over-think the answers. Please say the first thing that comes to you. There are seven simple questions. These questions may seem very random but they are not. They are general in interest, but your answers will help us to get a clearer picture of you. After I ask the question, you respond during the next forward swing you take. This will monitor inner youth. Please notice that the first test gets you in touch with the 'baby' side, symbolized by pure laughter or contentment, this one will deal with elementary emotions, and then the next one will be more advanced or rather your teen side. The fourth test will deal with more human-adult issues and the last one will be directed towards senior standards. Me personally, I find it very interesting that the age categories coincide with the growth categories, first vision then consciousness, then recognizing your own heart, then the mind and then last and most importantly, how much you've grown and how you relate to the universe and what allowed you to live a full life…Don't you find it interesting how perfect in nature it all flows?"

"Yes, I suppose you're right," said London. "I can see what you mean, but don't you think that there is a possibility for mistakes sometimes?"

Robbie, realizing that London was commenting on her own case and her lost information instead of his theory of perfect nature, was shaken back to the task at hand and requested that London try out the swing so that she could get use to it before they started. It was very easy to maneuver and London understood what he meant about answering on a forward motion, so she began to practice pushing to words out of her chest. Swinging back, all the way back, she took a deep breath. Then pushing her legs forward so the rest of her body would follow, she yelled out "Lobo" then swinging backwards she drew another breath, pushed forward and forced out the word "Iggy." 'Fine' she thought, 'I can do this,' so out loud she said, "Is that what you need? I think I am ready."

Robbie simply smiled and let London continue with a few more practice swings before he spoke. "Ok, Ms England, this is like your blotter tests on Earth, I say one word, and then you give me the first and quickest response that you think of. Got it?"

"Yep," blew London.

And so they began this second, quick and enjoyable quiz. Swing, swing, swing, swing, swing…

Robbie, "Playoffs"...........London, "Champions"

Robbie, "Holidays"...........London, "Baking"

Robbie, "Creatures"..........London, "Great and small," swinging higher to fit it.

Robbie, "Rebates"...........London, "Moola"

Robbie, "Reruns"............London, "Bugs Bunny"

Robbie, "Carnivals"...........London, "Taffy"

Robbie, "Fuel"............London, "Dale Ernhardt"

Robbie laughed out loud and said, "Great answers…And see, it didn't hurt at all."

London started laughing with him, "You mean that's it…There's no more?...That was so fun…Truly awesome…Where did taffy come from?...I didn't want to stop…Make up some more."

"Sorry sweetie, but we have to get on with the rest of the analysis," replied Robbie.

London, keeping up behind Robbie asked, "So, how did I do? Is it on to door number three for me? Everything is happening so fast. I am feeling better now. And maybe by the time we get done the April-Placer will be waiting for us with news about my going home."

Robbie began speaking about his next quiz, "Door number three will lead us to the Hearticheck. It will provide readings for your passion instincts. It will tell us where your interests are the strongest. What was once your heart beat, pumping human blood through your veins, is now throbbing all your energy towards your soul orb. London? London? Are you listening to me?"

She wasn't. She had stopped at the door to look at the room. It was completely opposite from the last one. Instead of dark blue/black walls, these walls were pure white. And instead of no furniture, this room was packed and piled with computer looking wall units. There was an oval slab of metal that was directly under the center of a see-through bed that looked like sky-blue Plexiglas. Robbie added further information, "Again, none of our tests are painful. For this one you don't even have to think or work. To get a proper reading we ask that you lay face down. This will allow all the intense and hidden energy to fall to the bottom of your belly, or frame. Everybody realizes that awareness comes from the brain, but not many people realize where their soul is located. It is near the bottom of the heart, towards the stomach. You have heard the expression 'gut reaction.' Well, that is your soul."

London nodded and replied, "Oh that makes so much sense. Easy enough, I am all yours. Let's get this show on the road. Is it like napping…Is it like meditation or what? Am I supposed to think of an object or color?"

Robbie answered with a negative, "No, just lay face down on the plextable and that plate, we call the stretchascope, will do the monitoring for us, OK?"

There was s small stool for London to climb on and then the rest was up to Robbie. London could see him attaching wires to the stretchascope but she wasn't really afraid since no part of it was touching her...And he did promise that all of these Heaven tests were to be painless, didn't he? After all, she was dead. Oh! Even thinking 'it' to herself sounded wrong. This all had to be a huge mistake.

Almost instantly upon lying down, the table began to move. The silver plate stayed in one place while she began to spin. It wasn't a lot, just about the speed of a merry-go-round. The centrifugal force made London feel like she was being hugged, squashed and held to the table... astronaut style. Round and around she went, never faster, never slower. Round and around. Round and around. She must have spun around

20 times before something started to happen. All the panels that were surrounding her began to respond. The sound was kind of like slow popping popcorn, yet it was tiny red lights that were blipping on and off. There seemed to be a hum in the room although London couldn't figure out if it was the bed, the plate or some other buzzers that she was setting off on the panels. The red lights began blinking twice as fast now. They seemed to be playing a tune that sounded like harpsichord music. And then, just as quickly as the last quiz was over, so was it the same for this quiz. London didn't feel dizzy or sick. She didn't feel bad or dead. All she felt was surprisingly calm, but still homesick. Hopping off the table she kept telling herself to hang in there…Stick it out and soon she would be home with Jim and Brandi.

Robbie was mumbling something to himself about how interesting London's quiz results were and that he was more intrigued with each one and that he was soooo anxious to see the results. London almost begged him to tell her what he meant. But, he explained that these were all just one small module working toward her final report and that there was no way he could give her a reading. Well, an accurate reading, without seeing the conclusions of her final two tests. With that he had pushed, "So it is off to your Mindopsy. What a treat this is going to be. Come on London, follow me!"

As they exited door number three and headed towards door number four, London couldn't help but glance at the desk, which was still unoccupied and unchanged. Robbie noticing her reaction said in a self protective manner, "London, do you know that normally we destroy records as soon as your earth sentence is complete? You have no need for them on the Heaven Planets and we have no need for them here. So basically, once a Returner, there is no going back to earth. What you are asking us to do is the complete opposite of that which we are accustomed. Someone will come with an answer for you, but it might not be the answer that you want."

Now, not smiling at all, London didn't direct her reply to what he just said but rather to the task before them. "As you said before, on to door number four, 'The Mindopsy' is waiting. Then I will be one step away from the real truth."

"London, I can hear in your voice that you are upset. Don't give up. You are doing splendidly. So far you seemed to be a well rounded individual. I am sure we will get specific coordinates if we can just get through these last two quizzes, OK?"

"You got the power" London sang, mocking the outdated disco song.

Grateful for the ease in her demeanor, Robbie said, "Atta-girl. Now let's get going on quiz number four."

Lemon yellow was the only way to describe the next room. The tall, bare walls were the exact same color as the ceiling, floor and furniture. This time there were two chairs. One towards the back of the room that looked like a lazy boy recliner and the other was centered directly under a beautiful orange umbrella. The cushion looked like an old fashioned lawn mower seat and the footstool looked like a mushroom. London spoke for the first time since they had entered, "Wow, this one looks like fun. Is that where I am supposed to sit?" pointing to the center of the room.

Robbie nodded, adding, "You can trust truth that this is highly effective and highly entertaining. It is the beginning that always gets the Returners going. Even though we are about to enter the adult cycles of your quizzes, we still hope that you find it as pleasurable as the first three. This Mindopsy uses the color yellow to generate pure thought. This one tests the length and strength of your honor and dignity. How you relate to heroes and bad guys. How you treated others and more importantly, how you viewed the universe and your place in it."

"That doesn't sound very fun that sounds serious. You didn't even tell me the results from my other tests yet, oh wait, yea, I forgot, the first one I giggled, so I am an active soul, the second one I had answers for each without stuttering so I am a well rounded soul, then you do the third one called a Hearticheck, but tell me you can't reveal the information yet. I miss my home. I miss Jim and Brandi. I miss my dogs. I don't want to be here and now you are telling me that you are going to test me on how I view the Universe and my place in it?"

"Please try to calm down London, I know this is all a lot to absorb, but truly it will help us get to the bottom of your true character data. I promise that you don't have to do anything but please have faith in me and the system to just relax. Take a seat and this will be over before you know it"

London, feeling like a first class heal for yelling at Robbie, did not say another word. After all, it was obvious that it wasn't his fault and he had done nothing but be kind to her. She finally took her seat in the lemon yellow saddle and tried to apologize with her eyes, but without warning, the base began to move. The seat began to shake and she heard her own laughing voice. She felt like she was four years old and getting a fake pony ride on someone's knee. The beat was very specific; Like a Rumba, but it was throwing her around like a rodeo clown…More giggles and more conga rhythms, da da da…da da…daaa… laughing so hard she just about fell out of the chair. London would try to lift herself straight and then the mushroom would shift, the chair would lift and she was thrown to the other side, da da da…da da…daaa. The sensation reminded her of shake and bake chicken commercials and old cartoons, which made her laugh all the more. And then, as abruptly as it started, it stopped. She turned around to apologize to Robbie in a proper way, thinking that the quiz was over.

Robbie interrupted her quickly, "Shhhh. That was only the beginning to stir up your mind. Concentrate. See the sights. Smell the aroma. Hear every sound and just let your mind wander, OK?"

London looked up and saw the machine lowering. It resembled a 1950's salon hair dryer, but much longer. It wasn't like the stereo headphones that she had imagined. It was like a body cast spanning from the top of her head down to her waist and it wasn't an ordinary headset or eye-visor because the minute it was in place and covering her, it was like the largest movie screen ever…Periphery vision deluxe, like a window to the world. She thought to herself, 'this would have been a wonderful invention on Earth' and wondered why nobody had thought of it. It was better than IMAX screens. The bright yellow of the room had disappeared behind this new screen and she found herself looking at blue sky. A blue sky so real that she felt she could reach out and touch the clouds that were floating by her captivated eyes. She floated from nature backdrops of different kinds and different types of weather until she recognized her exquisite Texas. Floating through the inland she came upon a country village, then suburbia and on to big cities. There were moments that her journey was, rather her visuals would, take her close to people, close to animals, close to scenes and situations that are so common…From a lonely child being called names, to a celebrity receiving kudos from the public. Other times she floated from nursing homes to big business then from a birthday party to a baseball game. It all seemed to be detached and yet it was like a world cruise in thirty seconds. The sounds and smells where so intense that near the end she found herself, once again, homesick. Robbie finished with scenes of animals, which had always been her favorite hobby in life, so she told herself to smile and this would all be over soon. Someone had to know what had happened.

She heard Robbie's voice breaking into her own thoughts. Pushing herself to be cheery, she said, "You were right. The whole thing was a blast. I loved the shake, rattle and roll in the beginning and I liked the mini-movie just as well. Can you tell me how I did on this one?"

"I can tell you that it was superb. Your readings are off the charts and now we just have one more to go so that I can compile all of our findings," replied Robbie.

"How long will that take?" asked London.

"What? The last test, or to get your results?" Robbie asked back.

"Both," London responded, raising her eyebrows for his reply.

"Well, the last test is the quickest of them all. And then your new information is projected to us immediately following, OK?"

"Ok, but let's check your front desk one more time," was added by London. "Maybe someone has left a note for you. Robbie?"

Chuckling under his breath, "Yes, Ms England, if your memory will serve you, we have to go back to the atrium to get to the next, and final door."

As she had expected, there was no one at the desk. There were no lights flashing, no sign of movement or new memos anywhere. Where they had left the icefood treats was completely the same.

"London, as you can see for yourself, no one is here. Let's go ahead with the Soulotomy, and then if he is not here by the time we are done then I will let you go with me to see if he has any news for us. Fair enough?"

Delighted with this new offer, London replied honestly, "More than fair," and then added, "Thank you for trying, and thank you for your patience with me. I am sure I have not been the easiest case for you, but it is just that I am positive that this is all a mistake and I am going to be sent home."

Robbie couldn't help but laugh, "Yes, Ms England, you have been somewhat of a mystery, but thanks for saying thanks. Your future is my goal." And then without need he added, "And I am beginning to be curious about you myself. It would appear that your name is not the only unique thing about you," he blushed.

"What do you mean by that?" London asked half playfully and half not.

"As always, time will tell, and right now I have taken up too much time. Let's go on to door number five, the Soulotomy. This is the last or senior part of our analysis. This deals with the secret you or the private you. It can measure your dedication to life. Not what you think about life, but how strong you are in sustaining life…Your longevity factor… Your survival smarts. The last section deals with 'if there was no one to watch you, what would you do?' Would you choose evil or good? And, could you survive trials and tribulations. As always, it sounds way more intense than it feels."

"How can you tell that? What do I have to do?" asked London.

"Just like the modules before this, our results are taken from inside of your soul orb. There is nothing that you can or can't do to change the outcome. Just follow your intuition and have fun. Let's go in, shall we?"

He reached for the door as London dashed around him, she wanted to be the first one inside, but she was stopped in her tracks. All of the rooms had been of good size and all of the rooms had been special in color or furniture. But this room seemed the biggest of them all, by far, like they were inside and outside at the same time. What caught London's eyes first, were the bright, bright, neon, rainbow lights that looked like the St. Louis Arc had been cloned fourteen times, dipped in fresh paint and aligned from one end of the room to the other. Robbie's chair this time was regal and high placed like a throne. The golden color was such an abstract from the neon that London couldn't help notice it, and the matching keyboard that seemed to hover in front of it. The whole room looked like a neon palace. London asked, "Where do I sit?"

Robbie followed, "You don't sit down in this one. You stand on the treadmill floor and then we run you underneath the lights until you light one up. That will be the category we focus on for you. Whenever you are ready just step up on the purple platform beginning mat and the machine and myself will do the rest."

From the bright gold captain's chair London heard him began punching and typing at buttons that were already lit up from underneath. Her thoughts rolled back to the planet Earth, loved ones and fun. Moments gone by and experiences that had animated her life. She had tried to enjoy each new day and had hoped that she had succeeded in helping others do the same. Awakened from her day dreams by the clicking of keys, she realized that Robbie's chair had risen to the top of the ceiling with his keyboard still in front and the clicking of his keys now sounded like chimes of heavy rain. Without a second thought she hopped onto the conveyor belt.

At first the color over her head was pure white when she looked up into the arc. It was like florescent bulbs in a doctor's office. But, as Robbie moved London inch by inch the neon bulbs over her head began to change and chime in unison. From white to a light chalky pink, from there to a bubblegum pink; On to magentas, then reds and purples, then to baby blue, true blue, green, aqua blue, night blue, then back to yellows, to oranges then shades of neon pink, neon blue, neon green, neon pink, neon blue, neon green, neon pink, neon blue, neon green, then every single bulb began to flicker and sing. London was so awestruck by the light show that she was trying to soak it all in, or learn the song or just memorize it like it was the last fireworks show that she would ever see. This, by far, was her favorite. She felt like she was in the craziest pinball machine ever made. She wished that she could run and dance and figure out a song by herself. She wished that Brandi could see the mechanical visual with her. If it were not for the fact that she was so anxious to get her results she would have stayed in there twice as long. All she was missing were some bells and whistles. Back and forth she passed through the tunnel four more times. Then as quickly as it began the room became quiet with a warm pink glow. Robbie was floating back to the floor and about to get out of his golden chair when she heard him whisper, "She must be a daughter of the Gods."

"How did I do?" asked a still laughing London. "Did I set it off enough? Did enough energy register so that we can get a reading?"

"It would appear London that you could light up a soggy log!" With that, Robbie explained that they were done. Her modules were complete and the only thing for them to do now was to go and wait in the atrium by the waterfall until the results were projected. London agreed. But much to her surprise, by the time she got off the treadmill, caught up with Robbie and headed for the desk, there were eleven other Placers in the lobby waiting for them. All were in white togas and wearing wide silver belts. London was speechless and it didn't appear that Robbie was expecting them either.

The April Placer slide-glided forward and began to speak. "March Placer Robert, we have heard your initial request for London's information data and we have watched with great interest throughout these proceedings. She has done extremely well, not just on one quiz, but ALL of them. It is the opinion of the Placer Panel, that this is a rare case of a kind soul being taken too early in its orb cycle. We have never and will never make a mistake with lack of information, but since this child has so much of it, we have no choice but to unleash her to the Heaven Planets and let them decide. We have observed that this particular Returner, London England, has all positive qualities and no negative. Therefore, the process of elimination that is half the basis of the test, is not working on her. In short, she contains pure and is all love. Her love for life, family and other humans is off our scales..."

London broke in, "Then why can't I go back? You just said 'early' and you can't find a place for me...then let me be a Returner to Earth."

"I am sorry Ms England. We deal with destiny, futures, moving forward. Do you see? We can't send you backwards. We don't ever deal with backwards, only forwards. It's the only thing we know. We PLACE Returners to somewhere new. It is the opinion of the January Placer that you visit each Heaven Planet to try to find which one would be best for you. Meanwhile we will keep your file, rather, what's left of it, and send it on to which ever Heaven Planet that you choose after visiting each one."

"This is wrong," whispered London, but she could say no more.

Hearing this, the July Placer spoke up, "Everyone feels that it is wrong for a moment when they arrive but usually Returners are adjusted by now. We have never made a mistake. We are willing to keep you in our sights until things are resolved because your happiness is what we are striving towards. OK? And, in the meantime you can discover everything that the Heaven Planets have to offer, and maybe even report back to us like an ambassador."

London thought, 'At least I still have a chance to go home, instead of them telling me flat out no.' Then she realized that all eyes were on her and waiting for a response. But, when she looked in their eyes, she was delighted to see bright ice blue angel eyes looking back at her. She wondered why she had not noticed before. It was like looking into the eyes of a saint. They were all smiling and humming and she felt true love coming from them. They appeared to be gathering and whispering just because of her, so she kept her answer to a very short, "Agreed."

London watched them stride-glided out of the room. They were comparing opinions on how beautiful and sweet that this London England truly was, and how did she ace every single quiz with flying colors and isn't it a shame that the girl won't be staying at the Interview Inn to become a Greeter herself. One commented that they didn't even know if she was male or female, but now that they had seen her thought that London Keni England was a perfect name for her.

London smiled herself back around to speak with Robbie, "You see that? No one knows where I am supposed to be because I am supposed to back on Earth, yes?"

Without answering her actual question Robbie said instead, "Well I am now done for this session and I guess we should make you comfortable for awhile  because we are still waiting on your final information compilation.."

"Why do we need it now?" asked London, "They said I get to pick a planet?"

"London," began a very serious Robbie, "You must concentrate. What they said was you are going to each and every planet. You must pick one in the end as your permanent space while stationed HERE, not, returning to Earth. We need the information to send on to the Heaven planets."

London found the resting place extremely comfortable.  At the moment she felt very tired and there were enormous white pillows in the entire left corner of the room. Fluffy white globes lay over her head like man made clouds and the softest lavender glow filled the entire place. Robbie had provided the standard white robe for her and although she liked it, she felt it a little bit too permanent...And yet, it wasn't her attire that was making her worry right now, it was the waiting. Why hadn't her Placer come back yet? What more could the tests reveal that they hadn't gone over already?  Locked in thought, it took her a moment to react when he finally did appear. Standing to greet him, she tried to brace herself at the same time.

"Give it to me straight doc." But, his non-expression made her add quickly, "Sorry, it is an earth saying. What news do you have for me?"

Robbie began quietly, "For the first time ever we do not have background data on a Returner. Usually, I have the opportunity to view the Earth history and then it is destroyed, what you call 'washed-away' then I go on with my quizzes and every thing just flows and fills in, but in your case the data has never came to me. I have checked with everyone possible but have reached dead ends. No pun intended. I should say, there was one unaccounted for transmission your day of returning, but none of it was legible. And I don't have your joyous memories to go by. For this, I am sorry ...The good news is that all of your exams here were very encouraging, they show you to be a logical, bright, flamboyant person with an excellent outlook. The other positive point right now is, because there is no precedence for this situation, we are able to offer you, as we mentioned before, the opportunity to visit each sector."

"Each sector?" asked London.

"I am sure that you noticed our seven suns when you arrived. Well, each one of those are a sector of rejuvenation. For each sun there is a specialized station, you would call Heaven, on this Heaven people are their most desired state, thus, filling up their energy form, thus becoming pure love, to pure energy…And, just like you should have remembered this, you should have remembered I have already explained, I can only move you into the future, there is no way for us to return you to your past. Our telelifts only extend up and out. We do not have the authority to send back a traveler…Ever. I am sorry London, but you can trust truth that you will know when you get to your Heaven, the Earth emotions will disappear and you will find true inner happiness, OK? Now, the Placers have all examined your quiz results and concluded that you're quite a diversified young woman. All have agreed that you can go, experience everything there is to try and then decide which station will be your final resting place. You will not need to contact us but we will be keeping a watch over you. We wish you joy and may I personally add this has been a tremendous pleasure to meet such a special Returner."

Dumbfounded, London stood quite still for a moment and then

stuttered, "So this is it? Our time is done? You still don't know why I am here and where I am supposed to go, so you are unleashing me into the Universe?"

Laughing Robbie replied, "Well, that's a little dramatic, the Universe? That would take more than your allotted rejuvenation time to travel."

"You KNOW what I meant. But, if I am hearing you right, it is my role up here to be a gypsy?" demanded London.

"Think more of it as a tourist, OK? You're just going on holiday." Robbie tried to change her mood one last time, and then unexpectedly, "The time is now for you to begin. Please, remember, it's not where you came from; it's where you are going! Follow me and I will escort you to your telelift."

# Chapter 4
# Merchandise Paradise

## Elle and LaWeez

London thought back to the crystal tornados that she had seen outside, they had seemed so far in the distance, but yet when they got to the Interview Inn doors there were all the Placers waiting to walk with them also. They looked like the holiest of choirs in their white, white robes with no other adornment than silver belts and crystal blue eyes. No one spoke words but the melody that was beginning to fill the air was like the most beautiful and peaceful tune that has ever been made. They had no instruments. The song had no words. And yet, the tone of their vocal chords and the vibration of their humming sounded like a symphony of harpsichords…Slow and rhythmic. Before she knew it, she was standing at the base of a beautiful see-through elevator. It looked like the outside was sprinkled with snow flakes and sugar. London turned to say goodbye to Robbie. She never really got to do this because he had already moved in line with the rest of the Placers and had begun to sing along with them. Still listening to the melody, as if almost hypnotized, she began rising in the tube and watched as the Placers became smaller and fainter, slide-gliding away. Before long, all she could see was light airy blue sky all around her body. As she floated up towards her first of seven temporary homes, she thought to herself that she should have asked more questions, but what would she have asked? She should have demanded answers, but what was she hoping to hear? You can go home. She should have tried to learn more about where she was going first, but it didn't seem like there was any time at all from when she was waiting in the Interview Inn to the Placers sending her on her way. She didn't expect a good bye party or anything but a little bit of outline or words to 'live' by would have been nice. Caught in her (own) self pity, London missed the first glimpse of color that was seeping down the telelift, but just as she rounded the next small curve she saw a kaleidoscope of neon rushing around all sides of her with Tesla coils zapping away in all directions. This too, was quite spectacular.

After coming to a complete stop, she exited the telelift and found herself at an enormous white and gold reception desk. There were two people behind the large black counter that held only one single gong that was fashioned after a huge shirt button.

The two girls spoke in unison, "Welcome to Merchandise Paradise." The one on the left said, "Hi, I am Elle," and the one on the right said, "And I am LaWeez." Again in unison..."We're your consultants on Merchandise Paradise. We believe that true joy is the combination of colors, patterns and design, in clothing, makeup, accessories and coifs. What we put on the outside is a true reflection of what is in the inside." Elle spoke next, "Excuse me for staring London, but I thought that you were going to be someone slightly different than you appear."

"How so?" asked London a little bit quicker than polite.

Elle responded first, "Well, it is partly due to the fact that your information was scrambled. I didn't have anything to go by except hear-say. It was rumored that London England, you, had been last years super-model for Ralph Lauren, and had eaten too many packets of sugar substitute and died of malnutrition."

LaWeez interrupted, "Elle, it doesn't matter, just by looking at her you can tell that she wasn't nineteen and yes, she is trim but not too thin. Anyway, the Knowledge Collectors sent word that her reentry information had been confusing, but she is very bright and loving. We need to let her orb fill here."

Elle agreed, "Yes, yes, LaWeez, you have got it all sewn up. I mirror your opinion." Turning to London, Elle asked, "Were you a designer or maybe an international buyer?"

London snickered, "No, my interest in fashion is in fingernails, I was a nail technician and then branched out to have PET POLISH, CLAW COLORS, and People and Pet Printers. I blended grooming animals with obedience classes. My business is, was called 'Pet-I-Cures/Woman-I-Cures.' Like it? My goal was to one day supply to all the dog shows and true animal lovers everywhere."

The two Greeters were very enthusiastic about London's business (which, surprised her) but told her it was time to go on with the rest of the orientation. Rising from behind their receptionist vanity and pointing. The three ladies began to walk through the smoke glass doors. This time it was LaWeez that began first. "Our station is set up in four main areas: Salons, Runway fashion, Custom/craft designers and Malls. We try to cater to each different variety of consumers. Different individuals are drawn towards different types of shopping and color expressions...Even males."

Elle continued, "When you get to your dressing room. You will find two outfits, one white and one black. On the top of your dresser in your dressing room you ..."

London broke in, "You have dressers in your dressing rooms?"

"Silly girl, your dressing room is your suite. It's your apartment or home until you leave here." Elle started again, "When you get to your dressing room. You will find two outfits, one white and one black. On the top of your dresser you will find 50 clothing tags, you can trade tags for any item on the station and you can trade any item that you have collected towards another one." Thus you can continue to experience new colors and styles which will continually fill your orb with pleasure, see? You never run out of changes, and you never run out of space from hoarding too much as in the style world on Earth.

You can go from shop to store to mall as you please, and you can wear anything you please. Amazing concept, wouldn't you agree?"

"Heck yes I agree! This is going to be a blast! I can hardly wait to begin and get out of this white robe. White makes me nervous. It always has because I always ruin it. Do I get a tag for this if I turn it in somewhere?" inquired London tugging at her toga.

"Yes, it fills and thrills me that you get the fabric and shape of the way things are cut around here" replied Elle, "You can go to any store you like."

"I guess my next question is where the stores are? How long are they open? Is there a limit on shoes?" London doubled up on her added inquiries, "Will I meet anybody that I have known and how long is my stay here?"

"Well, those are some good questions," zipped Elle. "There is a possibility that you could run into someone familiar. Yes, I suppose so, if they have reentered in the last five earth years and if they happen to be placed in Merchandise Paradise…Anybody specific that you are looking for?"

"No, it is just that malls were a major meeting place on Earth and I didn't know if it were true to form up here." said London.

As they walked through the slate grey tunnel and entered the shopping area LaWeez began, "Our malls here are four floors high and divided a little bit different than typical shopping centers. The first floor is nothing but footwear; the second floor will be skirts, pants and shorts only. The third floor holds all the shirts, dresses and coats and the fourth floor is where you will find all undergarments, makeup, accessories, scarves and hats.

LaWeez continued, "As you can tell, Elle has more complex taste, layered looks with deep rich colors, where as, I am more simple chic. Of course she would begin with the multiple-shops where as I prefer the art of a runway purchase. Aaahhh, the choices, the single attention to detail, the ease of just pointing at a walking example of beauty and saying 'make me look like that' now that is true heaven."

Elle cut in, "LaWeez, I wasn't trying to influence London, and I don't think that you should either. If you recall, I only started talking about malls first because that is what London asked about, by implying that they were gathering spots. I merely pointed out that it is all about the art here, not the acceptance of others."

"Well said! London will have to figure out her own style favorites and designs." said LaWeez, trying to save face.

They all three walked in silence. The walk took them past beautiful single colored, basic boutiques to multi-hued hippie houses that looked like they had been painted by 20 different people and then on past an entire subdivision of beauty salons and smaller shops. This is where Elle began to speak again, "See, these are quaint and quite attractive in their own right. We have a lot of Returners that want to be only here, or only in the custom fitting departments. It takes all kinds to make harmony. We find it most enjoyable and very enlightening." Just as the girls were finishing their tour LaWeez began to speak in whispers to Elle. London could have heard if she wanted but at that moment she was actually smiling to herself because she had noticed for the first time, some of the colorful and exuberant people around her. They were talking, laughing and some were even singing amongst themselves. Songs with fashion in them, "she was a tall cool woman in a red dress…" London noticed mostly women but a scattered few men were around also. Nearly all of them were smiling, chatting, pulling at or pointing to something that clad their bodies.

As London continued watching this fashion ballet she heard Elle's voice speaking to her. "London, we are being called back to our pedestal-vanity. But the message seems to be about you also, so we beg of you to come back with us."

Upon returning to the desk, they all three learned the message was about London. Elle explained, "Ms England, It would appear that your name is not the only thing special about you. The Placer for the Main Interview Inn has requested a special fashion show to be arranged for and by you. After trading in all your tags (one time allowed) you are to put on a fashion show for us. If we, the fashion family, find it stimulating then you will be moving on to your next Heaven Planet, OK? I guess this is the answer to the length of your stay."

London responded quickly, "You mean I will be organizing the entire show?"

"Exactly" The Greeters were already speaking in unison again and had returned to their positions behind the huge reception pedestal vanity. London, in a walking stunned state, turned to head for her new and temporary home heard the girls yell out "Go for what you know and ALWAYS trust truth."

So that is the thought that London held in her mind as she traveled from the girls to her dressing room. She would pick up her clothing tags and begin at the easiest part, the mall sector. Start simple and build from there, 'stay true to you,' she told herself as she browsed in and out of different colored racks. There were racks for each color both primary and secondary, but every piece of clothing on each particular rack was the same. The entire experience was so much more than she had expected. Fellow shoppers were friendly, the clerks were very helpful, everything seemed to scream her name as though she had picked out the patterns and styles herself and the most important change that she noticed was everything fit like a glove. The clerk had explained that by saying your size while looking at the tags it would make it a perfect fit completing all the alterations by the sound of your voice. London began to notice that each garment she would find was immaculate. No rips, no missing buttons, no stains or wrong colors. Her spree had taken her to each floor of the malls, browsing until she was sure that she had seen everything available. Then she went to the salons, boutiques, to have consultations with the true-self tailor designers and then finally slowed down to rest at the runway shows. London was very happy that she had saved this for last. There were plush, pampering settees lining both sides of the room. Chrome silver pillars appeared more like mirrors then metal and were used to be the base for the pastel periwinkle canopy that was waving overhead. There was an ever present stream of models that were stride-gliding through in smiling silence adorning exquisite costumes. White, yellow, pink, orange, red, blue, green, purple, grey, brown and black; one loop of misty colored models and then one loop of bold; one loop of plastic duds and then one loop of cotton, one loop of pleather and then a loop of wool. All in the same color rotation: white, yellow, pink orange etc. Even the ones metallically made (somewhere other than Earth!) London chose two outfits, had some angel food cake, and was off to her dressing room to go over everything she had gathered. Back in her changing room, going through her inventory London felt like she had everything that she needed and she was proud of herself to accomplish so much in one trip. Her ensembles were ready but she needed to return to the accessory floor at the mall just one more time. She had noticed a few shops before because of their catchy names like: Petite Palace, Dreamy Dangles, Savior Shoes, Supreme Scarves and Heavenly Hats. London decided that she would use the rest of her tags and then alert Elle and LaWeez that she was ready for her debut.

"GRACEFUL GARMENTS" was the marquee above London's runway. She had chosen the back patio of her resting place and had extended her runway out to the fountains in the rear. The refreshments were ready, the chairs were in place and the guests were beginning to arrive, and although she was nervous, London was also anxious to begin because the sooner it was over the sooner she might get to go home.

"Welcome and thank you for coming, as you all know this is my first attempt at fashion of clothing. My art form is fingernails and manicures. But, I hope that by listening to Elle and LaWeez, and observing all of you that I might have got the right idea…So sit back, relax and take a glimpse into what I think are truly graceful garments. I envisioned a wardrobe that was feminine with a tad towards tomboy trends. The first garment is perfect for leisure whether you plan to work out or run out. This white, pink, and grey combo is fitted with a real bathing suit underneath, with a wrinkle free skirt for the cover, its crisscrossed bra front adds added support, so the material can flow but your body parts stay tight. The bubble gum pink color says fun, the white says you're in control and the grey says, 'I'm tougher than you think.' YOU can feel confident wherever your free time takes you.

Moving on to everyday attire, I selected this yellow and orange gear. It has a white base color with a few red accents. This one is clean yet durable. The yellow screams, 'I have brain power' while the orange expresses individuality. The white base is non-offensive while the red highlights bring to mind a passionate personality." London proceeded with a little more confidence, "You'll please notice, no collar, which means no head or neck aches from stress. The sleeves are mid length to make moving uncluttered and yet have side 'wings' for support of the back. The knee length is perfect for bending and stretching. This too, comes with a sewn-in panel for optimum lift of body and mind."

The third model appeared and London continued, "Next is my personal favorite, we are such fans of the color black on Earth that I could not resist this pant suit. This all black pant suit will flatter any figure while allowing you to move in and out of various circles… Meetings, concerts and then to dinner after that. Perfect. The small lapels are styled to fit in anywhere, and are formal enough for any restaurant. The shortened long sleeves are perfect for staying free of soup bowls and yet long enough to not expose underarms. The slacks are loose enough to enjoy your meals and yet still tummy tucking, the sleek cut and design of the slacks will never be dated. You can wear short or tall heels. The lines of the jacket accommodate either. Most people would say that black is only for funerals and operas. A person like me, who inevitably spills something down the front of themselves, would surely disagree. Black is a blessing and with this outfit I don't have to tuck napkins into my shirt like a bib. This practical and chic pairing is the total package." London kept speaking of the fashion and over the mumbles. She could not be concerned right now if they were good or bad critiques. She was half way through and didn't want to stop.

"That concludes the practical portion of my show, so now we will venture into the fun or festive collection. The model appeared in an ice blue frock that looked like it had been made from neo-elves. The sweeping ice blue skirt was higher on one side of the waist then the other, sweeping down to the split that stopped above the knee.

The front looked like a pure diamond panel with an entirely empty back. The stiff shoulder braces kept the front in place and the shoes looked like they were made from the same materials. Truly a delicate, space age outfit and truly heavenly. This special wrap around was immediately well received by the runway audience. 'Now that got their attention.' London thought and with renewed enthusiasm, pushed on. This Merchandise Paradise stuff wasn't such a disaster after all.

"For my fifth selection I chose a solid tube gown out of space age material that will cover up the most flawed of bodies. I was instantly intrigued with this metallic fiber cloth. It is purple and teal blue, depending on the visual angle. This fabric will make you look like royalty, and an Olympian at the same time. The slate, silver choker brings the eyes up and towards your coif. It comes with removable sleeves, optional sash and outer jacket. This 'less is more' dress can be worn with any type of sandal or shoe and the majority of boots. Your mood will soar, as you enter the door in this one of a kind body art. Now for my last and most daring piece…This mimic-lingerie gown reverts back to a time of scrupulous romance…Tender hearts who wanted to be exclusively loved and devote themselves entirely to that cause of becoming split-aparts…Ladies in the living room and lions in the bedroom. This discreet dame can glow in the parlor with these golden threads woven with white soft gauze. The silky percale is thick enough to entertain family or close friends before the lights go out. When everyone leaves and once in the dark, the outer bodice is removed to reveal what would appear to be a very intricate tatting lace…but in fact, is 7000 glow in the dark stars that let off enough auras to produce an entire halo around you. With this lingerie, the look you get is angelic and graceful."

London emerged from behind her hiding place that she had been speaking from. She walked from behind the darkened patio to the stage lights and then from there to underneath the skylights and as she finished her jaunt in front of everybody she waved.

"I am London England and I would like to thank you for spending this time with me. I am hoping that you can see that I have learned a lot about form, color, patterns and fashion and that you, the judges, and the industry-community I hold in the highest esteem." In one burst, London could hear applause and laughter and people yelling 'adorable,' 'glorious' and 'most lovely.' Having heard this, she began to smile to herself because she knew that she had done alright and she was going to move on...To home...or another experience?

# Chapter 5
# Foodland Fanacity

## Steph and Fanny

Lime green clouds surrounded her and there was the sweetest aroma in the air, like London had fallen into a cotton candy maker. She looked down at her body, not sure what she was checking for, she couldn't see her feet but she noticed that she was back in her original white robe with the silver belt. She then looked up but there was nothing to see. Just more of the lime green clouds, she started 'swimming on land' to see if she could separate this friendly smog long enough to tell where she was. She knew she wasn't back on earth and was almost sure that she wasn't still on Merchandise Paradise, but no one had told her where she would travel next, for that matter, they had not even said goodbye. Everything was going so fast. London had begun to like Elle and LaWeez and would miss them. Why does everything always have to change so suddenly? She thought the same about Earth. Just when you get comfortable or content, then the winds of change came a howling. She was tired of guessing, so she began to call out "Hello. Can anyone hear me? Am I late? Hello," then she started to panic. They had said that her data was scrambled. Did she get really lost this time? And now she couldn't go forward or backward? What was she supposed to do now? "Robbie? Can you hear me? I think something has gone wrong. Robbie? They said I passed the fashion show. What am I supposed to do?"

"London? London England?"

Hey great, she still couldn't see anything, but at least this was encouraging so she quickly answered, "Yes, I am here, but I can't see anything through this green fog."

"You will, just wait a moment till it clears. It doesn't usually look like this but someone made a lime soufflé that has just blown up. Just a small kitchen fire, you understand. Nothing to close the cafe over," sounded the mysterious voice.

And sure enough the puffy green clouds began to rise in a light breeze and London's Feedergreeters were in plain view. The male spoke first, "You picked an exciting moment to join us..." his words fading as did his attention to the female companion who was standing beside him. She had a clipboard in hand that looked like every other home economics teacher.

The female began, "Hello, this is Steph, and my name is Fanny. Welcome to Foodland Fanacity home of all divine dishes."

"Foodland Fanacity?" London couldn't help repeat as an answer.

"Yes, we specialize in filling your spirit orb through creativity and nurturing."

Suddenly Steph interrupted, "London, on our original list there was only one London England. He was the inventor of no-calorie chocolate and non-stick peanut butter. Obviously, that is not you, because you are female. The head chef has heard your case from Robbie and will allow you to stay, temporarily, on one condition. YOU must participate in one bake-off that is officially judged and pass the final taste test just like everyone else."

Before London could answer, Fanny broke in, "Oh, Steph, don't be such a Frenchy, you don't have to scare the poor girl. She just got here, don't be such a rotten egg."

"I am not trying to scare her. She needs to be thinking about her presentation. We have to take her on the tour and prepare her for the bake off. I heard she did absolutely marvelous with her color and form, so I want to give her every opportunity now." Steph speaking only to Fanny had now turned his attention to London.

"Color and form?" asked London.

Fanny whispered, "Creativity."

Steph began to give her his full explanation. "The purpose of Merchandise Paradise, I presume, is to fill up orbs that crave color and form as their basis. They are actually part of your sight, senses and for some people vision is their strongest. Where as here," Steph took a long stewing moment, "I personally tend to think we have even more opportunity for sating and fulfillment. That is why I am so serious about my position as a Feedergreeter. Like on your last journey, we are just asking you to be true to you, be creative and listen to your soul and you can trust truth that your real personality will come out in the cooking."

Now turning to Fanny as if almost to test her like a teacher and pupil, he said, "Fanny, tell London about our four sectors, please."

But a second thought was crossing London's mind. Robbie had never answered her, and yet everyone mentions him. Could he hear her? Did he know that she had experienced and passed through Merchandise Paradise? No harm in asking. He said that she didn't have to physically report to him and that he would know of her progress, but he didn't tell her how or when she would be notified if they cleared up the mystery of her Returners data. No harm in asking. "What about Robbie? Does he know that I am here already?"

Fanny said, "Yes, when we checked in with our head chef, he was speaking with Robbie. We were told that you are just temporary until you choose the right, Heaven for yourself."

"Or I get to go home, right? They don't even know if I am supposed to stay dead yet. If nobody can figure out where I am supposed to be then I might get to go back to Earth. Just think about it. You didn't know who I was. You thought I was an old male chef who invented diet chocolate."

Fanny gasped, "Not low cal; he gave us NO CAL chocolate; there is a world between the two. Further I might add, that we have alerted the other Heaven Planets that you are coming so there might not be any more confusion...And, everybody knows that you are only a temp and trying to find your ideal place. We are your friends, not your captors."

"Thank you so very much for listening to me. I just wish I could get a straight answer from someone," said London, hoping that she had not sounded harsh or insulted her.

Just as if Fanny was reading her mind, Fanny stirred a little and went on. "Oh, you didn't hurt my feelings, this is the greatest place to be, and we want you to come back if that's what you decide. I wouldn't want to be anywhere else."

Steph nodded on behind them. As they began to walk towards the stainless steel city, Fanny began the tour guide. "To your right you will see four white stucco looking buildings, they are all resting places and you will be furnished with quarters and a galley kitchen, if you stay with us permanently. You have a fully functional kitchen for private experiments, but you are welcome to join a cater crew at any time. We don't have money or tags here. Your shopping list is your purchase power, so as long as you have it written down on something, you are given any kind of food you desire. Neat huh?" Without waiting on London, Fanny continued, "They thought of everything. For instance, notice that they sent you here next? What does every human do after they clothes shop? Go eat! So here we are and here you are." As they made it over a small little hill, London noticed that all the white stucco buildings were fading away and they were entering the biggest garden she had ever seen. In the distance she could see a copper colored farm house and a barn to match with an entire field of animals on the other side.

Fanny kept talking, "Foodland Fanacity is mainly four different sectors, this being # l, of course, because this is where it all begins, off the land. Healthy Heaven is what the locals call it, if you want food and cooking in its purest and oldest form, this is the place for you. Where as, Sector # 2, is just the opposite. Any fast food that you can remember on Earth is all up here too, in Sector # 2. And yes, they are still called Happy Meals! Sector # 3, is the cosmic cuisine, if you are craving something that is a delicacy, or even something that is out of this world, these people are the ones to see in Sector #3. And last but not least, on the contrary, most humans favorites... Sector #4: Deity Deserts. Surely not to be confused with Diet Deserts, These are D-e-ity deserts... Food of the Gods.

Almost forgetting that he was back there, London was startled when Steph broke in "Do you have any questions London? Do you know already where you want to study?"

"Thank you for asking Steph. You and Fanny have been very nice and very patient." London continued, "Food preparation was never one of my big points because my husband is a chef."

Fanny gasped twice, "London, Your husband?"

Fanny looked at Steph without saying anything, but he answered her like she had. "Maybe it is this mixed up data stuff, or maybe she has a strong mind?"

"What?" London pushed.

"Most Returners do not remember their past or the people they knew on Earth. Not in this phase. They say when you get to pure energy you are reunited with your split aparts. For now, time and space are supposed to be yours." Proudly, coldly, "I do not rehash my history," quietly steamed Fanny, her food motto pouring out unnecessarily.

London spoke up, "That's funny, I just used the term split aparts on Merchandise Paradise…And, not only can I remember his name, I remember his face, where I lived, my step- daughter, my immediate family, friends and my pets. How do you explain that?"

"We can't," spoken honestly by Steph. "But at least, since you are here, Robbie is trying to make you as happy as possible. Maybe they will find your perfect Heaven Planet and maybe in time your memories will fade…as distant as someone from your first grade classroom."

Fanny squealed, "Oh, you are always so gloomy, you go away now and let London and I walk around together."

"No, London has enough to do without you, and we probably have other Returners waiting for us already. No, London has to do this on her own," quietly replied Steph.

So off they went together leaving London to roam through beautiful fields, to small bakeries, through well lit fast food restaurants into the dimly, tree covered canopies of the restaurants to where everyone must end up their first day here, the deserts. And heavenly deserts they were. Cookies, cakes, tarts and torts, pies, brownies, fudge and puddings, with all flavors of icing, creams and confections. Nothing was missing and nothing was left out; the perfect accents of fruit, chocolate, cream and candies. After sampling no less than five different plates, London thought it best to return to her quarters.

The suite was comfortable, roomy and had a strawberry marmalade tint. It had a full kitchen to the right hand side. London thought it best to rest first and then go over everything that they had said when she could think a little clearer. How ironic that the first Heaven was fashion, which Brandi loves and the second Heaven was cooking, which Jim loved. London wished that he was here to ooh and ah her way out of this. He would put these chefs on their knees with just one barbeque. She wished that she had paid attention to him cooking. She couldn't just give them potato salad with peanut butter and chocolate milk, which are the only things that she ever made. Everything else was always handled by Jim Madrid. She had to concentrate. Steph and Fanny had given her the same advice as Elle and LaWeez…Go for what you know and trust truth. So, that's what London was planning to do. If honesty could get her through the fashion show then maybe, just maybe, it could get her through a bake-off. She had looked over their utensils and kitchens; she had studied every cook book and recipe that she could get her hands on. Now the timer was ticking towards the moment of truth. There were ten different tables and only two judges. London couldn't see any other dishes or chefs because all of their booths were filled to the rafters. She had heard that one entry was 14 different pancakes. One was a seven course meal, and one was a vegetarian victory. One was nothing but finger foods. One was dishes from around the world and several people had chosen to do 'native foods' of other planets. All the variety was starting to make her nervous and her own insecurity was starting to work on her insides making her stomach do belly flops. What if they didn't like it? Could she be fresh or just another left over? Was there a list of things that were mandatory? Questions, too many questions! She told herself to be still. She could see the two judges coming her way.

They stood before her and waiting for London to begin, they started jotting notes. Clearing her mind, London took one big breath and then tore the plastic sheet off of her display. The crowd was silent, the judges were speechless and London was left there holding the cover to one huge block of strawberry ice cream. It would have been a perfect three foot square piece of pink ice cream except for the top. It looked like the back of two airplane seats, or two seats from a theater row. The judges looked at each other, shrugged and began to walk away saying, "Maybe she didn't understand the assignment or how important this quiz is but..."

London cleared her throat to get their attention, picked up the big carving knife, which was the only tool on the table and proceeded to trim the bottom into the smallest of points so that when the judges looked back at it again, it was a huge pink heart. London took one can of whipped cream and drew a fluffy white outline around the whole thing. The crowd roared and London's huge pink heart stayed right in place and with perfect balance, it appeared to be floating in air. London said, "You told me everyone likes desert and the only thing I own right now is my own heart. Everyone has been so kind to me that I wanted to give a piece of my heart to all of you. I am grateful for all the experiences of life and I have always liked to try different cuisines, but nothing beats 'simple, cool and satisfying'" Thinking of Robbie, London ended her speech there.

The first judge said it was very tactile, the second judge said her display showed an artistic eye and how clever that this London proves to be. And the crowd? They went crazy.

"Oh, what a sweetheart this London truly is. Sweets for the sweet," added someone else.

"Very inventive to only be with us such a short time," stirred another.

London turned to Steph and Fanny, "Do you think it will be enough to let me pass?"

As always, snobby and stuffy Steph answered flatly, "I don't think it is going to win first place, but I have to tell you that no one has done anything like that before and I am hoping, for your sake, that the judges will take that into consideration. And in your case, you're being judged individually. No one else can change your fate. The recipe is orb filling, I admit."

Fanny chimed in, "I think it was dreamy London, and I heard a rumor that it isn't these judges that are deciding your fate anyway. It's really the head chef and Robbie that is very special, if true."

London wanted to tell them one more thing. "Please say goodbye to me. Don't let them whisk me away without telling me where I am going next, OK?"

Fanny answerer, "Remember, I told you we want to help you and that we already checked into your situation? Well, I can tell you right now that your next Heaven to hit is the Sports Sphere. Logically, after you shop, then eat, you should go work out. I know for sure that your next test will be of endurance and strength. How do you feel about that?"

London laughed, "Actually, I will probably have more success there than anything up to this point."

Fanny, "Well you did really well at this, your first bake off, and your other tough subject, fashion. So they are already over and the rest of your journey should be easy and fun for you."

"Sports Sphere, huh?" asked London one more time, "then what, I wonder?"

"Fanny, that's enough. You have given her too much information already, I know that you want to help, but you wouldn't want to scramble her up and make her stumble because she was thinking about two Heaven Planets from now. She has to concentrate on each trial as they come," brewed Steph.

"No sir. Sorry London. I just wanted you to know that everyone is pulling for you and all of us are excited and anxious to hear about your outcome. Trust truth and always follow the goodness inside of yourself and you won't go wrong, OK? Think about coming back here in the end," urged Fanny.

"OK, I believe you, and thank you for sticking around." As London turned to say a special thanks to Steph, she felt uneasy that he was already gone. And then turning back to Fanny, alas, she was gone also, replaced with nothingness. Just as quickly as she had come to this Heaven, she was floating towards her next. London knew that she was off again and she would never be returning to Foodland Fanacity.

# Chapter 6
## Sports Sphere
### Vic and Tori

She had felt the sensation of a lift off, almost like parasailing. Her toga/robe acting as her parachute, but she didn't feel like she was falling…More like hand gliding. The space around her was not dark and was not powder blue like the atmosphere that she was used to, but more silver-white than she would have pictured. She imagined herself traveling at the speed of light and engulfed in all the energy that was swirling around her. She felt massive and weightless at the same time. Maybe they let her see this journey so that she could lay eyes on all the different fields and arenas that she was approaching in her landing on Sports Sphere.

"Superior Sports" was in huge letters labeled across the biggest gym, but she couldn't see inside to see anything. She felt herself being lowered by a pulling force that was bringing her down onto the most perfect wooden floor that she had ever seen. It made her want to roller skate. She was not paying attention to the scoreboard, stands, hoops or other players. Because there were people screeching all around her as she landed at the far end of the building. Was she supposed to wait here, or head into the locker room with the rush of slide-gliders heading her way? As usual, she decided to wait…No need to take the initiative, she would find out soon enough. She began to scope out her surroundings through the dimming half-time lights. The roar had numbed to a hum, she felt a cooler breeze above her and no one seemed to comment on her presence. Surely they had seen her...Or, maybe it was common place on this planet? She had her first total awareness moment, "England? England?" She turned around and found herself staring right into an orange and white #23.

"Yes?" Looking up, she thought 'maybe I'm going to be a cheerleader' since those were her colors long ago.

The Coach answered for her, "Well, YOU are not seven foot one."

"No sir, I am only five foot two, answered London.

The coach explained, "Well they told me you were coming, but when I looked into my own files of recruiting, the only London England I have listed is an African-American from

Cleveland, Ohio, who was in the NBA, and was 7'1"...Too bad, I was looking forward to having him on my team." The coach looked down at the inside of his arm as if he were going to check the time, instead he had an entire sheet of information on his forearm. He made a few notes and was mumbling to himself when London cut in.

"Well, do you know where I should go or who I should see? This is where I landed and I want to get my proper assignment and get finished with all these games."

Coach barked out bluntly, "My advice would be to start in the Superior Sports building."

As he started to walk away, London chimed quickly, "Hey yea, I saw it when I landed, what kind of sport is in there?"

Shaking his head, walking away, he yelled back at London, "Women, of course, haven't they taken over every sport?"

At the door appeared Vic. His movements produced skip gliding. He began drilling her and then switched to instructing her all in the same sentence. "How was your entry? Was the coach very confused? Did he try to put you in at your height? Have you seen Tori? You will tell her that it was her conference with Robbie that made the opening minutes a disaster. She really dropped the ball on this one."

Tori stood two heads higher than London and was already laughing when she reached for London's hand. "Hi London, I am Tori. Robbie says good luck and God speed. He even added that all is well. So far, so good." London thanked her. Tori just nodded and kept on going. "You know...It is funny, we thought you were the famous London England from the NBA." Tori motioned for them all to begin and then spoke directly to London, "I'm glad that your Placer, Robbie, contacted us before hand, just for the little 'heads up.' We would have been shocked."

"And what about my team?" broke in Vic.

Tori was very calm, very collected and said, "For now, I think you should help Ms England in anyway that you can. We will get you another rookie soon. Return to the gym and you can keep the Olympic court for five more games. I will catch up with you later."

London didn't really see Vic's exit because Tori was already addressing her again, "You and I get to sightsee and fit you with a different uniform for awhile, we try to keep it simple, but you know how fickle leagues and players can be. By simple attire, I mean, all men-only sports wear blue. All girls' sports wear any shades of red, and Co-ed teams can choose between green or yellow."

"What about billiards? Do you have pool?" asked London.

Slightly stunned, Tori grinned at London and said, "Yes, and like every other sport here, you get to choose. Do you want to compete against just women or both men and women? And as if she read London's mind, she added, "We have a perfect mix of those that do and those that don't play co-ed. After all, this is Sports Sphere. All we have is superior sportsmen and women."

London liked Tori. She was commanding but caring and seemed truly interested so London was as honest as possible. "Well, I am starting to get the pattern of how all this is happening and  supposed to work, so if this planet is anything like the last two, you are going to tell me to be true to myself and go for what I know."

Tori laughed out loud so London kept going, "From the moment I first saw your beautiful Heaven Planet as my next home I have been thinking about my favorite sport. My hobby is animals I don't think that will help me unless I pick polo…Anyways; your planet is spectacular and is the most like Earth that I have seen so far…So much like Earth that it makes me think of Texas and what I did there with Jim. Some of our best times, other than the beach, were playing billiards. I think that I was pretty good. Good enough to help me pass this test, so that's what I pick."

This time Tori spoke lower, "You remember your loved ones?" London nodded but before she could elaborate, Tori spoke, "By now they should be just the name of a distant someone that you can barely remember. That is very interesting and makes your visit here all that more a different ball game. I have never heard of a Returner remembering so much, or for that matter, wanting to go back to Earth. Most are so bliss filled that the reason for everything is very clear and the three phases are no longer a mystery…So what does your data say? Robbie just said that you had many talents and options and we were to give you a comp ticket to anywhere…Box seats included."

Trustingly, London offered, "There's more. By the end of the visit, he will give you a test for me. I don't know how I am supposed to get relayed messages from him and my progress…and something about an ambassador…It's just the way it's worked so far."

This time Tori added, "I bet you are too bush league for telepathy yet." Both ladies laughed, London was just happy for a comedic break, Tori broke in "What's it going to be London, pink or yellow? You get changed and we will go exploring. I will show you where the tables are, and then I have to find Victor and return to the hoop section," nudged Tori.

London was pleasantly surprised that her new sports gear was a lot like the first outfit in her fashion show and it fit like a dream. It made her reflect on the last planet. She had chosen to remain in her white and silver toga. It looked enough like the other chefs gear to blend in with all the different cooking styles. She imagined that it made the appearance of her strawberry heart sculpture more enticing…Laughing to herself; she was snapped out of it by Tori. She complimented London on the fit and then asked if she was ready.

London said, "Where's the starting gate?"

Taking a deep breath Tori explained, "We have indoor and indoor extreme, outdoor which includes sectors for cold weather and cold weather extremes then warm weather and warm weather extremes. We give every Returner the opportunity to fill their spirit orb with endurance, strength, knowledge and power. Where were you before? Foodland Fanacity? That's only fun for so long, and then humans feel like they have to work it off. It's human nature…Energy that stirs within. We strive for spiritual sports here. Improving and rejuvenating everyday. All touchdowns, all grand slams, and all three pointers that are nothing but net. Starting to get the picture?"

Through out their time together the two ladies went from the gymnasts, to tennis courts, to ski lifts and then to mile high cliffs to watch divers and dare angels. This beautiful Utopia had surfing, golf, racquetball, darts, skateboarding, wrestling, la Crosse, polo, soccer, ping pong, biking and even gladiators. At the football arena, London stopped to play close attention.     Tori asked, "Are you a fan or did you play?"

London said quickly, "Oh no, but my sister is a huge fan of the NFL."

Tori gave information that London wasn't expecting, "She would love it here then. We have peewee, jr. high, high school, college, pro, arena, and my favorite, old school leather helmets. Those tried and true veterans play old time rules no holds barred. Knee stabbing, the head slap, the crack back, clothes lining, horse collar and even spearing."

"Oh," was the only thing that London could say because she hadn't understood any of what Tori had said.

They had begun to walk towards the business looking buildings when the hair on the back of London's neck began to tingle. She looked at Tori and whispered, "Did you hear that?"

"Did I hear what?" asked Tori, almost a little too coy.

London smiled, "You did hear it. It was billiard balls being released from their home tube." At the same time that she was speaking, she was peeking in the windows that were to her right.

Veering up to the steps, Tori said, "It would appear that you have chosen well London. You heard the first set to be racked." Reaching for the door, Tori added, "Shall we?"

London stayed by the entrance a moment to absorb everything. This pool hall sported four inch thick carpet, to prevent shooters legs and feet from getting sore. Three different heights of tables, all regulation size in width and length. There was plenty of chalk, straight sticks, and billiard balls that looked as though they had just been painted. The lights, those were bright enough to see by, but high enough to miss and no quarters necessary. No one seemed loaded or pushy or mad or crooked. London saw tables surrounded by red clothing and then some tables that were surrounded by blue clothing. Lemon-lime dots throughout the room made a beautiful rainbow affect. All the colors were very dazzling up against the glass bottoms of the tables then cut in half by the horizontal, cool white, velvet bumpers.

They played enough games for London to get it out of her system for the time being before going to meet Vic. Tori reassured her the she would be coming back here later, as she already had a locker (room) upstairs, for later. If London chose to come back here permanently and for her energy-understanding tournament that would probably happen right here in this sector. They passed through outside basketball courts and went further into the sector to get to the indoor stadiums.

Victor was smiling ear to ear and came over to them right away, "If you have changed your mind, there is still a spot for you," all three laughed out loud, but it was Tori who answered for her.

"I found her a sport, we found her a locker and now all we have to do is wait to hear from Robbie,." and then added, "She needs this badge of courage and we are going to help her get it. Got it?"

London left them to their basketball and went back to her locker. But instead of being able to rest, she kept thinking about pool, so she headed directly for the tables. She played straight pool, then eight ball, then all odds, then all evens. She practiced brakes, bank shots, cue ball tricks and of course, her english. She had decided to go back to her locker to rest, when she looked up and saw Vic first, and then Tori behind him. They both looked very serious so London stood straight up and said, "What's the deal? What's wrong?"

"Nothing," said Vic, "We just got the playbook on you, so we thought you would want to know right away."

"Yes, of course I do. But why so serious?" asked London. "Is there some kind of catch?"

Tori stepped in, "Yes and no. Do you remember saying that when you are outdoors you are usually with your animals?"

"Yea and?" asked London.

"Well, the good news is if…No when, you pass through this planet you will be heading towards Animal Eden," Tori half replied.

"Great, so when is my tournament," said an eager London, "And who do I play?" She added more like a question this time.

Vic assumed he should be the one to tell her, so without warning he blurted out, "You are going to surf!!"

London gasped, "What? Me surf? I thought I got to play pool?"

Tori touched her arm, "I am sorry London, I should have made sure with Robbie before I told you yes, but he says playing against someone is not fair in your case. These visits are supposed to be solely for you."

"Hey, but what about the bake-off? Wasn't that against other people? What about the other chef's that were there?"

"Yes, I already thought about that and asked him the same thing. He said, the other contestants had no bearing, on your finished project that would affect your fulfillment because you were judged individually. Imagine that you are taking your drivers license test on earth, there are other people around you and on the road, but they don't affect your outcome. Playing pool against someone else might change the perception of what you are supposed to enjoy. It would be a shared fate…" Tori didn't finish before London pushed.

"Well, I won't enjoy surfing, the only thing that I have ever done is Boogie-board with Brandi in shallow water." Screeching even louder London continued, "Oh, my gosh, I will never get home now! Boy, when you said badge of courage, you weren't bluffing... And when am I supposed to ride these waves?"

Vic looked down, and Tori got quiet, and London knew the answer, "Now? I am supposed to do it now? No practice, No lessons? And, I just played 64 games of pool for nothing?"

Vic looked back up at London, "Yes. Not only did we come to bring you the news, but we came to take you to the beach."

London, still in total shock, tried to think of Brandi, Jim and the only surfer that she knew, her Uncle Bruce. Nervous and stunned she said, "Let's do this thing, Hang Ten".        When they arrived ocean side there were just a few people. She was ever so grateful for the lack of on-lookers. She pulled off her mini-skirt then the over shirt. They gave her a bright orange board, so with her stomach in knots she waved towards Vic and Tori and was paddling out towards the biggest waves she had ever seen. It didn't look like the other surfers were even trying. They were just hanging out like baby seals. Once out there with the rest of them, they began giving her pointers to feel the waves suck the bottom of her legs out and then she could feel that the next curl would be strong. Once moving they told her to kick like crazy, hop and lift herself up on the board with one motion. They instructed that if she could do all of these things, and keep her balance, she should be able to ride it in to the shore.

Paddle, kick, hop and lift. Paddle, kick, hop and lift. Keep your balance, keep your balance, keep your balance, she was chanting to herself like a mad man. The winds came up, the wave came to her and she was gone. She remembered thinking to herself that things moved so fast up here on the board, and that she never got enough time to prepare herself, but at this moment she could tell she was holding her own. She could feel wind on her face and the water sprinkling her body, she told herself over and over again, balance, balance, balance…Ride the wave, don't get worried, don't think about the undertow, stay focused, think of your Uncle Bruce or all those surfing tournaments they had ran on television. Just stay up to find the end. As she was feeling a little bit more comfortable she had started to try to ride the crest, zipping to and from one side or the other, she was loving it and looking for the shore. It wasn't until it was too late that she saw the wave dying and felt her momentum slowing down. She worried that she wouldn't make it, so she tried with her own body to push forward. The first time it seemed to work. Yes, she was getting closer to the shore, but the second time that she tried, she felt the board jet forward just a little too much and before she knew it she had fallen off the back. She could tell that she had made shallow water because of the ocean floor beneath her. She could feel the sand against one shoulder and then it toppled her over and over and up and down until she had lost her sense of direction. In her own way of dry humor she thought 'Great, I am going to die twice, when I don't even remember the first time.' Trying to look up to find light, she felt something pulling on the back of her neck; did they have a hold of her hair? Is this the lifeguard? Did she fail? Would she have to try again, or find something else to do to move forward? She felt her head come above water, she could see light and before she knew it she was laying on the beach. She tried to stand up, but there seemed to be seaweed all around her legs. She tried to gather herself and in looking down she noticed that she was back in the white robe with the silver belt. Panic ran through her body. Did this mean that she had to start over? Once again, she tried to stand up and/or speak, but all her energy was focused on the force that was touching her face. She could feel pressure on the right side. Was someone kissing her cheek? Now that made her mind and her eyes come alive. What? It wasn't the lifeguard. Or even a human. It was a small animal…So, she had passed after all!

Her mind thought back to the last day of every grade school year when the children would be given the entire day for recess. Rushing from sack and relay races to field and track circles, and then on to jumping and goofier types of play. Laughing, healthy faces being herded from one event to another event so they could gather as many ribbons as possible. What was happening to her now? Zooming from contest to contest seemed to mirror those same memory feelings...Except she didn't want ribbons, or school to be over. She wanted to go home.

# CHAPTER 7
## Animal Eden

### ALEX AND XANDER

"What in the world?" She stammered. When she looked around there was a definite difference between this and the beach. She had surfed good enough to pass and now she had surfed her way to desolation. No people, no buildings and no arenas. No Victor and no Tori and no more surfers in the water just one little beagle puppy. London, true to her nature, instantly started petting and playing with the puppy. "Well, hello there little guy, looks like I made it after all. YOU wouldn't know where I am supposed to go would you?"

The puppy actually answered, "London, I don't want to startle you, but I am your puppy, Rabinjanatha. Do you remember me?"

London, in awe, looked closer, "Of course I can remember you. How many hours did we spend in your dog house after school and on weekends? I spent more time in there than you did. I guess I shouldn't be surprised that you can talk, at this point nothing should spook me, after all, times being as they are…Strange days. Hey, why did you run away?" asked London

Rabinjanatha wagged his tail and said, "The truth is, I didn't run away. I was taken while you were asleep. I missed you a lot and I want to thank you for always being sweet to me, London. You never let me or any other of your pets down."

London said thank you also and that it was good to know that she was well liked.

Rabinjanatha began to speak again, "Well, you had to be or they wouldn't have let you come here."

"Who Robbie?" asked London, still finding it hard to believe that she was talking to a puppy, and even harder to believe that Robbie wouldn't want her here.

"No, the council. There are only a few select humans that are aloud to visit our heaven planet, who we call V.I.P's…Vets/Important People."

"Oh I see, so you must know that I am a trainer and groomer on Earth?" London just had to ask.

"Well, No. Actually your data was a little scrambled; we thought at first that it was going to be a parrot named London England. The elephants were told by the gorillas of the mix-up, but they had remembered your legacy so they sent me before the snakes found out because they would ssseeee that you ssslipped or you were sssquashed. I volunteered to guide you. I knew that I had to come as quickly as possible. We have to get you to the main mountain, which is where you are supposed to meet the Trainer-Greeters."

"Who are they?" asked London.

The puppy answered as if he was waiting on that very question, "They are the primary servants for us. They had a wild animal resort on Earth and were known worldwide for their medical and healing facilities."

"And now they are servants for you here?" asked London.

"All of you are servants, both here and on Earth, didn't you ever think about, that? Most of us were 100% free to come and go as we liked. We choose our masters. Only the unfortunate ones that are caged are really prisoners. If animals are happy they stay loyal to one home.

If they are not, they will just run away the first chance they get. Thus, we own you, you don't own us."

London's response was filled with ponder, "Yea, I guess you are right. I never questioned it before because I was so happy to be around my animals…It wouldn't have mattered one way or the other, I would have still been as devoted to you. What is my purpose or mission going to be here?"

"I don't know but the Trainer-Greeters will. Let's go see what they have to say and where you are going to be placed from Main Mountain."

As Rabinjanatha ended, London began. "You know, everyone keeps saying that I am going to be 'placed,' but I haven't been 'placed' anywhere and I sure haven't rested. Just when I seem to get a grasp of one place then I am rustled away for a new mission." London got to her feet and as they left the beach and headed into the forest-jungle she began to notice all the animal noises that were getting louder with each step.

Rabinjanatha had begun to explain their Heaven Planet was full of every kind of beast imaginable. "We have every kind of animal here from ant to zebra; we have no buildings, no electricity, no manmade materials, but we do have total harmony, we even have some animals that you have never seen before…Animals from long ago and animals from different parts of Earth that you were never exposed to, as well as, some from other solar systems. All this and more without excess violence, for the sake of deep love and caring for living things and nature at its purest. Here you could fill up half your spirit orb on the love that you have already given us. There are rumors that you might get to work with the horses and their ponies that are just starting to stand and walk. You would like that, right?"

"You bet" was the only thing that London said right now, her mind was on Alex and Xander. Would they be nice even though the gorilla family had rejected her visit? Did Robbie know that this is where she was already and that she had barely completed the Sports Sphere visit? Would she ever get home to Brandi and Jim? Were they missing her?

Were they wondering about her absence? And what kind of experience could this planet put her through? A planet that was mainly only inhabited by animals? She could see the great Main Mountain before them, and when she squinted her eyes she thought she saw the opening to the cave near the very top. During the trek up there London saw foxes, tigers, bears, lions, camels, llamas, little, medium and huge birds...All kinds and colors of butterflies, then ground squirrels. When they got close to the top, London saw goats, gazelles and rams. As they reached a very jagged cliff London could see two blurred figures waiting for them. Rabinjanatha began to trot towards them so London did the same. She was expecting to meet and greet with them, but as London approached, Alex and Xander started to hike further up the mountain. She let out an unintentional reflex sigh to which Alex was quick to pick up on. He didn't comment to London but she did notice that he made eye contact with Xander.

When neither of them spoke, London tried..."I know that..."

Xander smirked slightly, without trying to be mean, "You are tired now? You think that we are almost there? We can tell by the way you looked up and sighed. The truth is that we have a long way to go. We are only at the foothills, maybe nearing the half way mark. The Main Mountain is very high."

"I can make it." Was the only answer that she wanted to give, because inside she was grateful that there was more time between her and the Council at the top. She didn't know what was waiting for her and she already felt like an intruder, so more walking was just fine with her. And at a seconds consideration she thought she should add more and sound more positive in the conversation. "It is beautiful country and this way you can tell me more about your animal reserve back in the States."

This must have been the trick because Alex and Xander both tried to reply at once. Immediately, Alex said, "Thank you London, you seem to be a ladybug of a gal. You would have liked our ranch. We specialized in saving circus and zoo animals, but also found all too often, humans would purchase 'baby' animals and then abandoned them when they outgrow the environment. We ended up with quite a few orphans. We had monkeys, bears, two elephants, tigers, horses and cats and dogs everywhere. We both had families, so that's lots of free labor…And me being the more gifted one, I home schooled the children for our wives. They both insisted on educational foundations for all the kids."

London broke in, "Do you remember them?"

Xander with another smirk "He doesn't and if he tells you differently he is a mule. Shortly after you return, your memory and Earth energy are drained so you can be fulfilled with a higher level of joy. You know that they are still living and striving, so that eases the loss and then after awhile, saying their names are just like repeating the alphabet. He just knows all the info because our lives were such public record."

His friend tried to defend himself, but it was futile…."Well, it is fun to pretend, but I will admit, after awhile it is just like saying the alphabet, no emotion there, see?" He said to London holding up his dry eyes and stern outdoorsy jaw.

"Well, I do. I remember all of my family and I am going back. That is my ultimate goal." London paused, letting each untouchable face of her loved ones to drift through her mind. "And, anything is possible, right? I mean, if the animals have an entire Heaven to themselves, surely that shows miraculous wonders are all around us and I am going home when this is all over."

"Jeepers, you have a one track mind," snarled one of the guides within her hearing range.

With such a deep sentiment being said they all silenced until at last, they had finally reached the top. London wondered out loud "Is this my final destination?'

"Yes. Now the great one in the Main Mountain will decide your fate," came from underneath matching safari hats.

London asked, "Does Robbie know? Is he here? Who is the great one?" Now London was very curious and began to pick up the pace of her up hill climb. Before she knew it they were at the doorway of the cave that she had seen from below. Alex walked in first. Then Xander and London followed trying to make her eyes adjust to the light. She tried to focus, but what was consuming her now was the slate smelling air surrounded her. The cave was very clean, almost like a brand new basement, yet smelled like Dracula's vacation condo. Grey was the only color that she could see except for the thick marble conference table and the tan uniforms of the entire panel. London tried to squint to see if she could tell who the 'great one' was. Was this going to resemble something out of The Planet of the Apes? However, they all seemed very equal and very civil. She was just so relieved that the room wasn't filled with wild animals waiting to pounce on her. Instinct made her walk towards them and will power made her stay quiet. She had decided to wait for Alex and Xander to talk. It was a good plan because someone was beginning to rise and as her eyes began to adjust she had to rub them one more time to make sure that she was seeing the 'great one' for who he really was. Marty, Marty Stouffer...The only man she ever wanted to marry as a child. Oh, besides John Travolta...She was chuckling over her own inside joking when Marty spoke in his oh so Marty voice, "Hello London, and welcome to the Wild Heavens, I hope that you are enjoying your outdoor adventure on Animal Eden."

London stammered, "Yes. Yes, it was very exciting, thank you for asking, and if could I just tell you one thing, sir. I have admired you since I was three years old. You and your brothers were ssooo brave. I know all about your first camera; that you left home at an early age; and you spent your first summers and money observing, not changing animal habitats. That's what I like about this place so much, no electricity, no buildings, only nature and a perfect planet, for animals to live without fear..." Now noticing the other panel members, London smiled.

Marty broke in and began the introductions, "Seeing that you're an animal fan London, you should know everyone here, but let me go down the list of each panel member as to not slight anyone, OK? OK" Marty proceeded, "On the end we have Eliza and Dr. Doolittle, then comes Diane Flossy; to her left is Jane. On the other side of me is Marlin Perkins, Jacque Cousteau, and Jack Hannah. On the very end is Steve Irwin." They all said hello to London. She made a small bend of respect and waited for Marty to finish.

"London, what we would like you to do is in your own way and in your own words, speak from your heart and tell us why you think animals are so important; and secondly, the kind of energy fulfillment that we strive for here is deep love and caring, tell us if you think you belong, or do you think something more exciting will bring you inner joy?"

London thought for a second and said, "Even when I was growing up I would rather be with my pets than people. I don't think we should be asking why animals are important. Maybe we should be asking if one species (humans) should be more important than thousands of animals. Animals aren't the ones destroying Earth, we are. Animals deserve nirvana…Animals are heroic and deserve recognition not extinction. I have more photos and photo albums of my animals than humans, also. Besides just plain respecting their right to life, I love animals because they are interesting, loving and fun."

London thought that would simplify things and be enough for the council, she didn't want to sound like a know it all in front of some of the leading authorities on animals…What she didn't expect was their silence. Not one of them seemed satisfied with her answer and no one was replying or giving her follow up questions.

"That's it? That's all you have to say?" asked Mr. Perkins. "No runaway tiger or cheetah in your closet as a child?"

London made herself remain calm, "All along my Greeters have been telling me to be myself. Well, the one thing that everyone knows about me is that I love animals. I thought that it would show through or you might have some history on my case. This is the place where I should feel the most comfortable and yet I have felt like a fish out of water since I have arrived. I didn't think you wanted me to elaborate. I thought you wanted me to keep it simple and short. Oh, there is one more thing that I should add. I hate to speak in public or defend myself, so I don't know what else to say. This is a very hard thing for me to do here. I have always found it easier to relate to animals instead of humans, and now I have to explain to a human why that is…Odd, isn't it?"

She already regretted the outburst, but knew it was too late to take it back, she just couldn't believe, of all the planets to feel bad on, she would not have expected it to be ANIMAL EDEN. This, of all subjects. All she could do was wait in silence. Instead of the next movement being from one of the Council, London saw little tadpoles moving from behind her. One by one they were making their way towards Jacque Cousteau. He was staring at them so hard that London could tell he was actually listening to them, he told the rest of the council that these tadpoles had come to them on behalf of London to say how she had saved them from a mud puddle that was drying up…Lifting each one up with a spoon so safely and to a bigger creek edge. All three ladies on the panel couldn't help but oooh and aaah. They made London feel a little better about her current situation.

Following came the tadpoles a group of frogs, telling the judges that they were the ones that London refused to dissect in school, and went back after class and set them free. After the frogs came the birds, possums, squirrels, rabbits, skunks, raccoons and one ferret. All of which were healed and given a new chance at life by this one small child. Next came the clan of the strays; beaten and hungry kittens heralding the name of London England. Everything became very quiet except for one small buzz. Flies were swooping down to Marty squeaking, "She never said 'shoo fly' to us, she was the only one to treat us decent, try to feed us and give us real names, she played with us for a long time… And, she would let us crawl up and down her arm until we had all the salt we needed for our larva."

Into the room ran a band of mice, all of which agreed that London was the greatest. "She gave us her cheese and oatmeal. When our mother lost in a cat fight, London kept us safe in the floor board of her bedroom until it was warm enough for us to go outside." One little solo puppy hobbled up, "I thought I would never walk again…Not only did she let me eat her popsicles until I felt better, but then used the sticks to fix my paw."

As the puppy was finishing up with his testimony, in came a small parade of reptiles. There were small, bright green garden snakes and a couple of boa's...

"Enough. Enough" said Marty. As he turned to London he proclaimed, "London, you truly are a horse of a different color, and if you would like to come back here to Wild Heaven's ANIMAL EDEN, then we would love to have you. Your very own cave will be waiting. In the meantime, I would like to thank you on behalf of all of us, and all of the animals, for your love, awareness and generosity in the past and for your patience now. We hope you enjoy the rest of your adventures. This is when we say goodbye, but hopefully we will see you before the next hibernation season. We will see you next time on ANIMAL EDEN."

"What do I do now?" asked London.

Marty answered, "All you do is walk out of the cave. When the light hits your face you'll be in a new place."

London turned to all of her pets saying goodbye to each one and them. She hugged Alex and Xander. The very last thing she did before stepping out the door was wink at Marty and said "Thank you for having me. It has been fun..." And then she looked out into the bright light that was supposed to take her to another planet. She walked towards the opening, looked down unto the beautiful valley and then back up into the light for a final time, and then she was gone.

# CHAPTER 8
# Amusemetropolis

## ABBY AND GAIL

What lay before her now was almost indescribable. She wasn't looking down into an endless valley anymore; she was looking up at towers of carnival lights. AMUSEMETROPOLIS was written in a thousand tiny stage lights above her head and although there was a gate there, there were no gatekeepers…Just tons of balloons. Her eyes were already moving past the entrance and into the parks when she heard the voices of her Treat-Greeters for the first time. They were giggly and hyper and yelling in unison, "London?" Running towards her, they each shouted, "Hi, we are Abby and Gail. Welcome to your next Heaven." As they got closer they reminded London of little bumble bees. They had basic black shorts and light yellow blouses. Their voices were very similar in tone like singers from the same family. London waved and waited for them to get to her. When they did get nearer, London noticed that Abby was carrying a set of clothes.

They got to her and handed the outfit to London, "Hurry. Put these on. We are going to have so much fun. This is the best Heaven of all and we can't imagine anyone wanting to go anywhere else. They say that we are all the 'peter pans.' That is why we are so pleased to have you and that you are going to pick us!! If you want to fill your orb with positive energy…What better than pure joy? That's what we specialize in; true, laugh out loud happiness."

Gail interrupted, "Less talk, more walk, get her to the changing rooms so we can go play."

London was sandwiched in between the two girls as they made their way through hoards of people, it was a little hard to get used to after the space and seclusion of ANIMAL EDEN. It seemed as though everyone here had just heard the funniest joke. So much smiling and laughing that London had missed what Abby was saying, so she asked politely, "I am sorry, I didn't hear you. Could you repeat that?" Abby echoed, "How did you like Cirque de Soliel?"

London nodded, "Oh yes, I know them. I have seen three of them. Is that where we are going first?"

Gail squealed, "No. Remember? We are going to the changing rooms."

London, "Oh, then are we going to the Cirque de Soleil? I like them very much, that would be fun."

Abby said, "Stop playing with us, we know you were a star with them."

"Who? What makes…? Where did you get that idea?" asked London.

"Aren't you London England, part of the famous high wire act?" said Abby.

Gail pointed to a doorway, "There, you can go change in there and we will be waiting for you…Whoever you are."

London laughed…These two girls were like Tweedle Dee and Tweedle Dum, with not a care in the world. When she came out of the girl's room they were debating where to start. It was London who spoke up, "When we used to take Brandi we used to start with the big major rides before the lines got too long; calm down on some fun, mild rides; eat a little bit, and top off our whole trip with the water sections. That way we didn't have to walk around all day with wet feet."

"Great plan," said Abby.

Then Gail was quick to add, "Yes, great plan. That's what I have been trying to say all along…Big rides first, water last. But, let's ride everything twice!"

Again in unison, "Let's get started."

The huge lavender doors were large enough for all three to enter at once. "Your name IS London right?" whispered Abby.

"Ah yes, but everywhere I go they've seemed to be expecting a different London England. I am from Alice, Texas. I had a family. I had a dog grooming and obedience training school. I have never been a circus performer, and I have never been to Canada."

"Oh," Abby remained whispering even though London's voice had been louder than her own. "Then you don't want to be here? Are you afraid of rides?"

A calmer London replied, "No, I am not afraid, but I didn't actually choose to come here. My information was scrambled when I Returned. My Placer, Robbie, is having me visit each Heaven Planet while they are trying to figure out where I am supposed to be. If it doesn't come to light by the time I finish each Heaven Planet…I am hoping to go home. They, the Placers, say I get to go where I want to. Well, I am going to keep asking to go back to Earth. They say I have to stay here and choose which Heaven Planet that suits me best," added London without reason.

"That's starting to make sense to me," finished Abby, but more interested in the rides.

London thought about how serious her situation was…How it didn't make sense at all and yet she felt a little lighter just being here with Abby and Gail. They had such positive outlooks and they didn't seem to care about any rules, formalities or what was taxing. It didn't seem like they were concerned with anywhere else but where they were now.

London, looking up at all the different rides thought to ask, "Do you know what my test is going to be? Has anybody mentioned a quiz for me?"

Both girls assured her that they didn't know, so London added, "No? So far nothing? I didn't think as much. If you didn't even know who I was, then I shouldn't have expected you to know anything about my fate," fading as the girls eyed their destination.

"Sorry," but not sounding it, both girls grabbed each of her arms and then Abby reflected, "Enough of the serious stuff, we like you just the way you are and you can stay as long as you want. With us guiding you, you may never want to leave," Abby spread her arms open wide while she was talking, which made London start to notice all of the rides around her. They were right in the middle of the thrill seeker sector. Gail insisted that they go on the stand-up coaster first and then it was decided that each girl would take a turn picking which ride came next. The first coasters were wooden and metal type tracks. They had round spinning rides and scary creepy rides; there were glass houses, moonwalks, whirlybirds, terror trains and log rides. There were old fashioned sectors that had carrousels with benches, merry-go-rounds with wooden animals, flying bobs, cages and the tilt-a-whirls. Just when London didn't think she could take anymore it was Abby who said that she needed to rest.

They went to get some cotton candy and then ride some calm rides for awhile. All three headed towards the sweet smelling air and then relaxed under a fake tree and a blue plastic bench. London thought she should ask one more time, "Say, this has been great fun and I have had a really good time, but on the other planets they would have already given me a spirit search quiz by now. I know that you are all about fun and games and everything but think hard…Are you sure you don't remember hearing anything about what I should do when I arrive on Amusemetropolis?"

"Nope, we don't know" quipped Abby.

"Nope, we don't care" added Gail, "All we do is have fun and be joyful (not) Sorry."

"Why should we know about such things? Tests are not merry." trying and failing to debate, mumbled Abby.

But like no conversation had ever been started, Gail began again with the child-like urging, "Come on guys, less talking, more walking, let's go to the Goldie-oldies."

Abby said OK to Gail, and to London she added, "Here we don't have resting places, when we get tired we go to the picnic lodges, and no one has ever given me an assignment for you or anybody. But, if I hear anything about a quiz for you I will let you know."

"Can we go now?" Asked Gail, who was already heading back towards the tilt-a-whirl without waiting for their answer. "I want to begin right where we left off," Gail called over the edge of her shoulder.

London and Abby made a stronger effort to catch up with Gail and as they did, Gail began to speak rather quickly, "Then, I want to see the puppet show. And it is right by the fun house with the funny glass mirrors. And I want us to try our luck at the fish bowls, OK? I want to win another flat, aluminum clover leaf necklace, and then we are going to try the ring toss to get a colored walking stick and pick your age and guess your weight, too. They give you a pencil box."

All this was done and then completed a second time. As they walked out of the Laser Light Show, London noticed the midway was right in front of them, the girls decided on the bumper cars, then the scrambler, the swing rides, the parachute lift and to London's surprise they even had the umbrella cups!!!! London stopped in her tracks, backed up two steps and stammered, "No thank you. You two ride this one and I will wait for you at the exit."

"Oh no, why? You can't be afraid of this one? You have gone on everything with us so far, this one can't bother you," questioned Abby.

"Yea, what gives?" doubled Gail.

"I am not afraid. I just don't want to go on this one. I will rest." attempted London.

Abby broke in gently, "This is Amusemetropolis. Nothing is going to happen to you. Just trust truth, and us, enough to reveal what is wrong."

Pausing, London admitted, "Well, I didn't remember until now, but once, when I was little I went to the Sweet Corn Festival in my home town and I rode this ride. It caught fire. It was dark already and I remember seeing flames against the night sky. All I could hear were popping bulbs from the heated neon on the sides of the carnival ride. I thought my end was near because they were not going to be able to get us all off in time, but all of the crew kept working and miraculously none of us were hurt. I am not afraid now; it's just that I hadn't thought about that for along time…Maybe this is my test."

"So, see? No time like the present to face your fears," jumped Abby.

All three girls got to ride together, at first London was nervous, but by the time they went around about five times she was laughing and enjoying the breeze in her face. London was so relaxed when the ride was over that she felt proud that she 'rode it out' and thanked the girls for helping.

For the first time Abby seemed even bubblier than Gail. She said, "Oh, that's fine," and then abruptly started screaming, "We're going to the water rides, we're going to the water rides. We're going to the water rides…"

And that they did. They went on slides and splash flaps, tubes, bouncers, bubblers, the tunnel of love and the submarine sinker, through the lazy river to the puddle pond. They were soaked, roaring and happy.

Gail insisted that they revisit each and every ride until the end where they went through the waterfalls to get to the barrels, then on to the inner tubes and when they got all the way through the park and they came to the enormous finale, 'THE SUPREME STREAM OF AMUSEMETROPOLIS.'

They were heading towards the biggest, fastest, wettest coaster that has ever been built. All three girls were excited and silent. As they piled into the front row, it was Abby who mustered the bravery to say, "This never gets old…You better HHOOLLDD on London." As the last girl, London, sat down, a big vat of water dumped over all of them.

London squealed, "Hey Wow, did I trigger that? We haven't even left the gate yet? And they get us wet…Cool."

"I know, isn't it great?" wailed Gail back at London.

Just as Gail finished her response the boat pulled out of the gate. London was speechless, the speed of the ride took her off guard, she had imagined it to be calm at first but it wasn't. It zoomed away from the gate like a monorail. More importantly, when they left the neon canopy of the gate, they weren't staying in the park sector; they were headed into a forest. The ride was very loud and very exciting; they went through miles of trees, in and out and up and down mountains, through sunny meadows with millions of flowers to acres and acres of grape, date and palm trees. This amazing little speed boat took them through white water rafting ripples that dumped them into the middle of a desert.

London saw one small oasis that was taller in the distance. She could see twenty or more taller trees. There appeared to be some kind of a tent or cottage built on the other side from the stream on which they were traveling. London could see one tall silver pole…Maybe a flag pole.      Like a horse running back to his barn, the small boat revved its engine and doubled its speed. The girls cackled louder as they were splashed in the face by the spray of the waves, they seemed to be going faster and faster and still be picking up speed. As the girls' voices became one steady scream, down and down they dove. It was the hugest, man made water slide that London had ever experienced. Down their desert stream they went.

As the oasis grew nearer to them, London heard Abby yell out, "It's almost the end of the ride, smile for the camera." London tried to tell her OK, but she couldn't get the words out because she was breathless with joy. As they approached the lens, London looked up, tried to smile and click!! Flash!!!

For a split second, London thought, "Whoa! That's was a strong camera bulb," but then she realized things were different already. She wasn't wet, she wasn't outside and she wasn't with Abby and Gail. 'What happened? Was she at her next destination already? What had the test been…To laugh again on the umbrella rides…To make it through the rapids? What was the quiz? The girls were so care free that they had never gotten around to serious matters, so here she was back in limbo, she didn't get to say goodbye (or rest yet) and now in another strange place. Where was she? And where was Robbie or her Greeters? It seemed like he had abandoned her three planets back. What would she be discovering next? She knew she was indoors because everything was so dark, but all of her attempts to see were to no avail. At the moment: blackness only blackness, she rubbed her eyes and in turn tried to adjust her pupils. In a mild voice she cried out, "Hello?"

The voice that answered her did not sound familiar. She wasn't even sure it was a person because it had sounded distorted and had only been one, quick sentence. "Time to relax. Fill the mind, fill the orb."

# CHAPTER 9
## Video Utopia

### ZACH AND KARI

"Where am I this time?" There was no verbal response to her query, but yet London could tell something was changing around her. Across the room, there began to appear two rectangle windows. They were horizontal, side by side, and beginning to illuminate with a glowing purple background, similar to black lights. There was a person in each booth, but London couldn't make out their faces. As the room became lighter, London could see her own hands and body. Looking down, she saw that she was now in a one piece slate-grey body suit that had a metal collar around her neck. She reached up to touch it and found it was smooth, comfortable and had small sockets on the right side of her neck. This made her both cautious and curious. What would happen on this Heaven Planet?

"Hello?" She tried again.

"Greetings, Returner. Welcome to Video Utopia. The power-up process is almost complete then we will begin your previews."

"Who are you?" London asked for a second time, "What is going to happen?"

"I am Zach, the Sound Greeter. In the other console we have Kari, Visual Greeter."

"hEYE" mic'd Kari."

So London answered back, "Hi." (Except, in the correct pronunciation.)

In the next moments, there were magnificent colors flooding the room, like a tornado they swirled all around London's head. She held her breath in as to control herself. She tried to sink down in her glowing, lit, green chair but there was no where to go.

Zach beeped in, "Please don't be afraid. That is just 'Ms all-seeing Kari' doing her projection run through…She thinks that sight is the most important layer. I think that hearing is your primary sense."

By this time the colors were a funnel cloud, three foot from London's face. It was actually amusing to watch them spin. They were combining, separating and then began to spin again. And just as quickly as they had manifested with one small melodic tone they lifted back into the floating mini-camera vox that was overhead.

"Connect." Kari said in a very robotic manner.

"Me?" asked London, pointing to her own chest and neck collar at the same time.

Zach was the one to answer, "No London. Hang in there. She was talking to me. I have to do my presets now."

Kari shrugged her shoulders at both of them and looked back at her buttons. So London looked at and waited for Zach.

"You'll find that she is very sweet, but one of very few words. All she cares about are eyes. vids. eyes. vids and what the eye can see." Explained Zach and without a breath went further to say, "The word 'connect' meant it's time for my sound check. After she gets her run through, I have to add and loop the audio to what she has already programmed. That is why I said presets…Not that your fate is predetermined…Make sense? This will be a little loud at first, but your ears will adjust quickly."

London knew what he had said, but at the moment was picking at her Barbarella type clothing, so…BOOM came a blaster BOOM.

Three octaves lower than middle 'c' BOOM. The sound remained for a short amount of time and then rose higher in pitch until it sounded as if London's ears were ringing. Then the sounds, tones and pitches were intermingled and stuttered, low, loud, quiet, and then high. The computer played the entire scale: do, rey, mi, fa, so, la, ti, do.

Then a voice could be heard, "Check 1. Check 2…Synergy, Synergy, Synergy. Check 1. Check 2…Trusssssst…truth. Trussssst truth. T.T.T. Truth, Check 1. Check 2." The room went completely black. The new voice began again. Clearly, it wasn't Zach's, and she was almost sure that it wasn't Kari's. It was an avatar, a generated voice that was very monotone, yet pleasant.

"Video Utopia, where you fill your mind to fill your orb." As the presentation began, a small overhead camera vox came down and floated above London's head. It was projecting hologram pictures that were both life size and colorful. "VIDEO UTOPIA is complete with seven sectors of specialization:

The 'Oneder Sector' is for the absorbtion of any information you desire from annuals for basic technologies to encyclopedia of higher learning. You can become familiar with many different languages and most importantly, anything musical.

Our 'Second Sector' contains short videos in animation, art, documentary, exercise, independent…And as always, all things concerning music.

'Threeatre Sector' houses feature and full length works. You will find silent films, talkies, white and blacks or techno colors. Subject categories include: comedy, drama, family, love, non-violent strategies, and of course, every musical ever made.

'Fourward Sector' deals with all small screens: Including current news, techno reports and updates, new releases, classics, how-to tips, education, historical tales, musical workshops and musical performances.

'Fivestar Sector' is the virtual reality area and is truly the utopia in Video Utopia. There are terrains of every kind possible. Destination choices can entail fantasy, mission, learning, life-contemplations, and any type of musical ambitions that you may have. Compose, record, produce, edit or review.

'Sixle Sector' connects true gamers with ultimate technologies in sight, sound and realism. With its full variety of artistic, educational and fun programs to adventurous, foreign, off land and alien sections. The appeal is never ending. Choose to participate or choose to be a spectator. Any game ever imagined and invented: Including an annex for all pseudo-musical contests and concerts.

'Sector S(h)eaven' is all audio. Learn by listening or entertain your ears. This is the home of every musical archive in history: Biographies of artist, songs, videos and all available movie soundtracks.

**Pause and final instructions** It will be necessary for you to choose your favorite genre at the completion of your orientation. Your station will be recorded, your studio loft will be assigned and your collar sockets will be fully programmed for your clearance to invent, create, duplicate, transfer and receive transmissions. We, again, welcome you to Video Utopia and encourage you to take the hoverboard tour before making your final decisions. If you have any further questions please direct them to your Greeter Technicians."

The vox quit reflecting images of the sectors, the voice turned into a quiet new age melody, the lights went to low dim and all London could see was the neon violet purple of the control booths. No one in them, she wondered? Zach and Kari weren't behind the glass or their consoles anymore. London looked around in all directions and saw a door behind her opening, Kari smiled and waved to her and so London got up from her light green florescent chair and made the scan of the room.

Zach, behind Kari said, "Come with us. We are going on the hoverboards."

London noticed that Kari had on the same type of bodysuit that she was wearing so she commented, "For a moment there I thought I was going to have to surf again…lol.,,haha!"

Kari said, "The net? You will…" with a most puzzled look on her face.

"No. The ocean," London said, but by the look on Kari's face she was compelled to add, "Oh, I am sorry to confuse you. It was a joke about my last adventure. This outfit resembles the suit I used on Sports Sphere. Is this what you wear all the time?"

"Yes." Kari answered without any other unnecessary words.

Zach, in his plain, slate-grey shorts chimed in. "We here on Video Utopia concentrate on filling our minds. Fashion and excess material are not focused here. It is said that the first creators of techno began this tradition back in the 1900's. We tell lore of the mother of vids, Madonna, caring only about improving her craft. Diligently working to the point of stripping down to her underclothes rather than be restricted of movement or her creative freedom. Thus, all outerwear has been adapted to this basic gear, power source included. The material collects solar and your movement energy, the collar coverts it to recycled-usable energy. The nano-science of it all is mind blowing. We want to be as enthusiastic about our projects as those who came before us. We devote all of our time to be a tape head and a tape body technosaturates."

London snickered to herself but didn't want to explain so she commanded the serious side of herself to 'Think originality and creativity; Think serious thoughts. Think.'

Quickly London dubbed in, "I think the suits are fascinating. I love the color and the collar. I am very anxious to go outside and go hovering. Thank you so much, to the both of you, for guiding me."

When London walked outside the dark purple room she was surprised to be standing in a dome. Although she said nothing, Kari was the one to lead them to the glass door which led them to another smaller dome that was also glass. It was reminiscent of a porch; Zach started to explain the hoverboard to London. Left foot forward, right foot rear, acceleration under left toes, brakes under the right heel. And although there was no speed limit, Zach explained that there was a height limit. This made London wonder but she said nothing yet.

Kari walked outside first, followed by Zach. Exiting last was the right thing to do for London. Because she was so astounded with the view, it stopped her in her tracks and she almost dropped the hoverboard. She looked back up at her surroundings in awe.

The whole surface looked like it was covered with see through bubbles. There were different sizes and heights, but every structure that covered the planet were domes. Out of the top of each dome protruded an upside down icicles. Some were pastel pink colored and the remainder where a light gold. A thin strip of silver was attached to a small ball at the point then wrapped around the icicle antennas, similar to a slinky, until meeting the top of the domes. High above the antennas there seemed to be a constant mist of silvery flakes. Zach explained that the antennas were color coded by basics: vid or audio, and the metallic rain helped the transponder signals to travel at a faster pace. The sound that hummed above their heads was that of harmonic chords as if it was played on the frets of an acoustic guitar.

Zach and Kari had already boarded their hovercrafts and so London focused and moved quickly. She didn't want to be left behind. The most surprising thing to London was the lack of others. She expected to see more of the Video Utopia residents. When she asked about it, Kari quietly laughed.

Zach was happy to help her understand, "If a Returner wishes to be outside, they would travel to Sports Sphere or Amusemetropolis. What receive are die-hard electronicas."

The three hoverboards sailed them through blocks and blocks of studios, arenas, stages and sets. Zach pointed to a small dome toward the end of their tour and added, "We took the liberty of setting up your studio loft. If you have noticed, we have made one big loop and now we're back to the center. Your studio loft is here, in the mid-hub. You can access any genre from here, but there is still the programming of your collar and the matching neck collar for any animation that you want to create."

"Oh, is that what my assignment will be? Animation?" asked London.

Zach slowed his hoverboard down to be next to London so he

could correct her, "We are all artists here. We don't have assignments, we have projects."

"Sorry," said London with just enough time before Zach continued…

"Listen. I heard your reviews from Earth. They said you were the best computer animator there. I assumed that you would have a few things in your file that you would want to download and complete."

London wailed, "OH, another mix up! Listen Zach, I have never done that before in my life. I am a dog trainer and groomer and you got the wrong London England. I am London Keni England. I am just here on a travel pass from Upper-Anaheim. My Placer was Robbie and there was a bad scramble of my data. When I first got here everything was very confusing, and to tell you the truth, I am just as confused now…When really, I am doing everything I can in hopes of getting back to Earth."

Kari touched Zach on his neck collar, and then Zach spoke to London.

"Let's hover down a moment, OK? Center above a corner and check if the coast is clear and then travel straight down to land. Do not mingle in the transmitter wave region."

He made one sharp curve to a corner and then dropped out of the sky, instant and heavy. Kari followed him to the corner, and then used the one across from him. London, close behind them, got her board stopped and then realized that Zach had picked this intersection for a reason. There was a four sided ATM machine. Kari greeted London but didn't speak…Just opened her eyes very wide and smiled. London assumed that she meant what a great ride they had and lots of wonderful stuff to see, but she didn't have any way of really knowing what Kari was thinking.

It was Zach who spoke, but only to say, "Please stand by." He and Kari both unsnapped the small black bracelet that was around their right wrists and both Greeters walked over to the vid booth. They moved up close, underneath the clear awnings, and then proceeded to snap one end into their neck collars and the other end into the machine, the window before Kari lit up and started replying in a series of dots, musical notes and tones. Zach plugged his in and the entire screen went to numbers zero and one. They were getting the same link in different formats. It was Zach that reacted. His speech became increasingly rapid and systematic. Any unknowing listener would think it was different dialects of alien speak, only in a computer voice. Nothing as he had sounded previously. Kari's eyes never blinked and never left the visual code. The IMs went on for awhile and then simultaneously the session was over for both Greeter Technicians.

They returned to where London had been waiting. Zach, of course, was the one who addressed her. We at Video Utopia would like to extend our sincerest apologies. To us, this is the very worst thing that can happen to an individual. To have your records in disarray is disastrous in our world. Identity scramble, loss or theft is not a laughing matter. He continued in earnest. "I have already tried hackers for you. We have data for a London England and it is a woman, but she is from Silicon Valley, California. Her middle name is Penny, but that's all that's coming up for her. I think that she is too young for any post records yet. No other matches were found for someone coming here by that name. Do you want another technician?"

"No." said London, pausing and contemplating if, and how, to explain. "The name isn't the problem; it's the time of death I think. I came here too early. I was only 37...and healthy." "Robbie said my info was scrambled." added London.

"Yea. We have already verified everything you claim with Upper-Anaheim. I mean, they told us specific information based on your travels so far, but we do not know your past...Or your future. You are more than welcome to complete an Indy Project here. We will help you in any way we can, starting with a change of collars if that is what you wish. We, better than any other planet, understand the resoluteness of scrambled information." Zach had been the entire voice and then ...

"Useless" Kari added.

Much to London's surprise that the female Greeter had offered any words at all... But what a mouthful she had said, with just those two syllables.

Zach concurred with Kari and then asked London. "So what's it going to be? What would fill you with the most pleasure?"

London thought intensely for a moment; about spending hours watching Bugs Bunny cartoons on Saturday mornings and holiday cartoons seen year after year. Her mind wandered to weekends filled with slasher movies and the Twilight Zone marathons. She thought back to the Children's After School Specials, which reminded her of happier times and 1000 different sitcoms. In the end, after much consideration, she gave her answer slowly. "Well, during your overview I noticed that every sector had one thing in common, music. I am from a musical family and can play three instruments, so I think that's what I would like to do best. Besides, music truly is the universal language, right? No matter what race, class or homeland you are from. Every culture has food, love and music."

London could tell that Kari liked and respected her answer and Zach was so excited that he hugged Kari, lifting her off the ground. Kari tapped on his neck collar.

"Oh, right." Zach acknowledged at the same time he replaced her to her original spot. "London, we have to program your collar for optimum signal receiving. Thank goodness your studio loft is centrally located and is fully equipped. You won't have to be relocated and you won't want for anything. When you see this place, you are going to be very happy indeed."

London whispered to herself, "Seeing Jim and Brandi," but was unheard by them.

"Sorry to say you won't actually get to rest yet. Because the nature of your visit, there isn't really anytime to waste, is there? There is a project deadline associated with your production. We have to have the slotted amount of time to see the process, outcome and the chart ratings," added Zach.

"Huh?" asked a stunned London.

"Your vid has to hit," shot Kari.

"?" this time, no words came from London. Just an open mouth and gawking eyes ...everything agape.

"Way to go Kari. You have locked up her system." accused Zach and then turned to London to redirect his attention…"Sorry she was so blunt, but Kari's right," softened Zach.

Finally London could manage, "Hit? What chart? What other instructions do I get?"

Zach stayed with his softer voice, "Very specific. Since you're dropping down on a comp-ticket and whatever production you create must be a chart topper."

Kari bumped him so Zach added, "I mean, It must hit number one on the viewers poll."

"Great," was all a panicking London could think or say.

Zach let her absorb the information and then added, "We will take you to your studio loft now. Kari has already signaled ahead for your new collar to be waiting. There is ice and cream food for you. Also being provided is enough blank memory sticks to fill three projects. When you are finished, go to the Arenadome so that we can show everyone your premier."

"How will you know that I have finished? How will I know I have finished? How will I know when I have done enough?" sprang a naive London.

Zach popped off coolly, "Kari has cameras everywhere, and she will probably be the first one to see you leaving your studio loft." Kari smiled but said nothing. Winked at London and then suddenly pointed back at the dome they had originally assigned for London. The three riders zoomed back up to the travel lane and then headed for the entrance of London's studio loft. Once inside, they programmed London's neck collar to sustain two more sockets for tone clarity in the audio layers. The Greeter technicians said goodbye and wished London good mind vibes.

Looking around, London decided she would have fun with this huge recording studio, music store and sound stage all rolled up into one. She found her memory sticks, ate some icefood and headed towards her five computers. They had stacks of keyboards beside them and colored screens overhead. Each had their own typing board including separate headphones hung overhead from the ceiling for each one. Everything was electronically tuned and had perfect tone. She found massive web sites dealing with fractiles and mathematics. She found old school instruments that were programmed at the touch of her fingers like harpsichords and lutes. London didn't even know how long she had been in the dome. She just knew that she had discovered a whole new world of electronics and technology that she would have never experienced if she had not been sent here. For the first time, since her travels began, London could see the benefits of new discoveries. She had stayed content with her life. It was a good life, but now to explore a subject that was virtually unknown to her was eye opening. No. Soul filling. She knew music, but not like this. She had filled her life with outdoor, animal and family activities, but had let her musical childhood talents fade away. She pondered about the amount of time that she had spent looking into her own lens. Suddenly, she finally felt finished. Feel it, see it and believe it. No time like the present.

London headed for the Arenadome and tried to cease herself from panicking. The lines going into the arena were long and winding. She had a sense that they were all summoned to see her vid. Could Kari have gotten the announcement out that fast? Yes, London suspected that she could, or maybe they had the audience on stand by.

As she expected, Zach and Kari were waiting for her at the turn styles and led her down some stairs and back stage. Zach whispered, "You have to preface your project. Go out there, speak clearly and trust truth that it will be received as positive energy."

Copying some board meeting, London went directly for and clear up to the mic'd podium and began to speak. "Thank you for coming. My name is London Keni England. I have produced a music video for you and want to express my sincere appreciation for your attendance." Feeling a little bit more comfortable, she continued, "Normally, music is created first and then visuals are secondary. I, on the other hand, wanted to take Kari's approach and go for the visual basis first and then add audio. I encourage you to relax, be content and remember how times have changed on a global, local and musical scale. So without any further ado, I would like to present my project, 'Twelve Twists of Technology; A visual journey through history.'"

The video began on the big stage screen with the quiet hum of their own metallic rain; Rhythmic, harmonic and beautifully simple. The picture was of their own unique domes and antennas. Their whole silver, pink, bubbly world, right in front of them, with their own type of music soothing the back ground. The pictures changed and as they did, so did the music. Underlining the whole tune was their harmonics with a techno tone. Soon the audience could hear the layers of the song become lighter and fainter. The screen was entirely covered by the image of one antenna. The cameras eye followed sound waves out into space, beyond this planet and several others until landing on a distant constellation. This constellation was no ordinary one. It was a seeker of smaller worlds…Ready to merge with the next group of stars to come its way. The audience was about to see an extraterrestrial tango. Swirling smoke, asteroids galore and non-light were filling up the canvas before them. As the images became more complex so did the melody. The crescendo was being brought to a very dramatic volume then BANG; one slice of crescent moon in the midst of nothing. The camera scans to the right and at once the planet is seen.

The music begins again as the view zooms in way slower than it had zoomed out from Video Utopia. This view was of lava and tar pits, forests and caves, whose nomad residents were dancing to primal drum beats. Instead of depicting struggle and wars London chose to follow the progress of music. She displayed peasants from long ago staying rooted on small farms. Inventions of instruments and the nonstop creative process of sharing with others and of collaborations developing; people that went on to open schools, symphonies and stores. London followed the other breed of gypsy bands that had spread the seed and need for music everywhere.        After sounding quite ancient the harmonics descended into a lower key that could manage clear tones. Old world songs were being replaced with new world tunes. Imagination and drive was an ever present ingredient which led to larger productions and operas. London was very careful to only show performances of truly talented artists and the best arias ever recorded, both male and female. She took the audience from folk beginnings to big band sounds. Electrical equipment entered onto the scene and twisted morph style into a flowing, Bjork type number. It had been very easy to switch to the high pitched monologue of present trends. This wasn't ancient tempos anymore. This stuff was complex and intricate. She had traveled from classical genres to American bluegrass which led to old country and its cousin, rock-a-billy. London showed pace setters and classic artists, shakers and legends; from hippies to hard rock to disco and punks. All were represented.

When it was time for the grand finale, London took one more, deep, silent breathe and crossed the fingers of her right hand. The New Age Bjork number was coming to a close when all of the additional back ground music ceased and original harmonics were the only sound left except now they were louder. It was the melody that had accompanied the opening scenes of Video Utopia. Flashes of neon lights and their own metallic rain engulfed the arena and on the screen were silhouettes of technosaturates dancing in domes; each looking at a wall with cubed, multi-screens of hundreds of other technosaturates dancing to the same song...Connected by wires and hearts. All in all, London was very pleased with this chronological composition and hoped that they would be too. London had worked hard to learn all of the equipment in her studio loft and then had spent a lot of time at the music library gathering all the tracks that she needed. She had been surprised that there were no books or films available, and yet the amount of space that it took to house the entire history of music was as large as five traditional libraries. There were numerous rows in one direction, all of one type of music, joined to an entire wing of another type of music, which broke off towards more huge annexes. Instead of file cards containing Dewey decimal systems there had been a telejuke music center that had read her desires and emotions and pointed her way by lighting the floor beneath her to guide the path. This unique library had made her research so much easier than trying to find material on line. London allowed herself an inward smile and then refocused on the stage.

With the final note came explosions, then darkness. The entire stadium rose to their feet. Thunderous clapping and sporadic laughter told London that she had done it. At the very least, she had entertained them. She waited backstage with Zach and Kari for what seemed forever.

When the results came in London couldn't even look at the board. When the meter on the wall began so did Zach, "Number one in imagination; Number one in originality; Number one in artistic skill; Number one in style; Number one in music; Number one in visuals aaaannnnndddd Number one in production.

Relief set in with the knowledge that she would not be expected to complete any other projects. As the curtain closed in front of her, she noticed one closing behind and around her. And just as quickly as the relief had set in, so did the awareness. She knew that Video Utopia was history and this was her final curtain call. She had been through enough already to know that she was not going back to her studio loft, not saying goodbye to Zach and Kari, and didn't feel any closer to Earth. London was back to floating in darkness and mystery.

# Chapter 10
# Mechanic Majestics

## Nathan and Thaniel

In the darkness London could make out two voices around her. She tried to gather her thoughts and hearing. The first sentence that was clear to her was startling.

"Time for some noise, lets rattle this baby up."

What followed was the roar of a very loud engine. London had seen a sonic motorcycle at the drag races once. She had also worked on the tarmac for Delta and had heard jet engines fire up. Neither of those even compared to the noise that she was hearing now.

She found herself screaming, "Hello? Hello? Can you hear me?"

She squinted her eyes again trying to make out any outlines of her surrounding. Moments later she felt someone flip the helmet visor that was covering her eyes. She felt silly for not realizing this was the problem. Once the visor was lifted London saw that she was in a garage. The male Heat Greeters were on either side of her. They were in white overalls with name tags on them. One read Nathan and on the other was Thaniel. London smiled and waved, but said nothing; knowing that they could not hear her over the roar or the engine that was still filling the room.

Nathan, on the other hand, began to yell, "Greetings Returner. We are so revved up about having you as a crew member on Mechanic Majestics. We got the key to fill up your hot rod heart; we specialize in hands-on talent and coordination." Laughing more to himself than her, he went back to his work.

Thaniel walked over to the sports car that they had been tuning up and turned off the motor. When the roar was gone London was able to comment. "What a wonderful place you have here, thank you for having me. It's been a life long dream of mine to be a race car driver, long live NASCAR. Maybe for the first time they may have my info right."

Thaniel, who was on his way back, said, "Yea, It will be a big difference from being in a submarine."

London thought, 'Oh my gosh, I guess I spoke to soon. Here we go again,' so she said, "Excuse me, did you say submarine?"

Thaniel responded, "Of course, we have seen your history."

London tried not to pull an outburst, but she heard herself say, "Look, I wasn't a submarine captain, and if you want me to drive one I can't! I am not officially part of any crew. I am just a spectator who is traveling on a temporary pit-pass. This has happened to me everywhere I have been. Each planet has had me down as somebody I am not. I never realized there were so many people named London England!" She stopped because she felt the embarrassment and shame on her face. She hadn't wanted to come off as a hot head.

Nathan looked at Thaniel then back at London, "Now, who are you and why are you here? You're not here for the big meet?"

She calmed herself and replied, "My name is London Keni England and they sent me here from Video Utopia. I have been traveling to each Heaven to try to figure out where I am supposed to be because my information was scrambled and no one has my right data. If you ask me, I should be sent back to Earth to return to my family because it wasn't my time to die."

"Impossible." added Thaniel to the conversation. "No one goes back to earth, it's a one-way track; our roads are only one-way streets. Forward. Not backward."

London looked down at the overalls that she was now wearing and said, "I guess that's left to be seen and up to Robbie."

Nathan said, "Sounds like she just wants to do a couple of trial laps."

Thaniel agreed and added, "Then left's get going…time's a wasting and waits for no man…or woman. She seems like she's on the road for somewhere important."

He walked over to the port door, slung it open and said, "On your mark, get set, let's go!"

Outside there were garages by the score. The only things that broke them up were the paved strips. Nathan took over the explanations by listing all of the choices to London. "Here on Mechanic Majestics we have go carts, on and off road bikes, new and old cars, vans, jeeps and trucks; drag, funny and oval track racing. Aero travel includes single engine, jets and helicopters and lastly, we have water propelled vehicles also, like jet ski's, speed boats, cigarettes, sail boats, (with engines) and yachts."

They traveled all over the planet in Nathan's pumped up humvee. The one thing he failed to mention to London was monster trucks, so when she asked about, them, both men got silent and then it was Thaniel who spoke. "Well, that's a new one. We have never had a female want to go to that sector, but one does exist. We could go check it out if you'd like."

"Please," answered London, "They have always been a favorite of mine."

"We have them but they are a little different. Here we combine monster trucks, demolition derby and racing. Not only in the same arena, but in the same event." said Thaniel.

"Sounds fun," said London, "Let's do it."

Once inside the monster truck stadium, the noise took over their conversation. Nothing was being said, but London didn't mind because she was totally fixed on what was happening on the track. She studied their driving styles, their turns and their jumps. There were a. few crashes and then a few fender benders but mostly just racing. When it was over and the three of them were exiting, London spoke up, "That is what I want to do while I am here. Can you arrange it?"

Thaniel replied, "Yes, of course, we can arrange it, but are you sure that is your preference? Most 'Shirleys' like the rails."

London's thoughts went to Jim and how many times he had taken her and Brandi to the Sunday monster truck rallies in Dallas. "Yes, I am sure."

Nathan spoke to Thaniel, but meant for London to hear also, "Let's go back to the garage first and try to get the diagnostic readings on her situation. Then we will see if we can't make this monster truck thing happen."

"Good plan," smiled Thaniel.

The three went back to the original car port, then into their offices and turned on the meter reader that was in the corner of Thaniel's room. He punched in several bits of London's stats then sat down at the desk to wait for the machine to do its thing. The outcome was simple: London could be a part of the Monster Truck crew but she was not to race against other drivers. She would instead have to complete an obstacle course in a certain amount of time. Instead of doing trial laps she would be doing time trials.

After reading the information and terms, he handed it to Nathan to read over and looked straight at London and asked, "Do you accept?"

"Sure" she said, thinking to herself that the obstacle course sounded easier than racing. This one thing might be in her favor. If not for the fact that she wasn't putting up a pink, she was fighting for her future; her brother had taken her four-wheeling enough to handle this.

"Since you won't be staying for the total orb fulfillment period we are not going to assign you a rest area yet. There are few, and far between. But you are welcome to utilize the pit-stops at the track if you'd like," explained Nathan.

London agreed to this also and then asked Nathan and Thaniel if they could drive her back over to the monster truck sector. Once back at the raceway London was given her own huge, white monster truck with a big blue ~17~ on the door. Nathan and Thaniel told her that when her countdown approached she would do five trial runs and then the ten official laps would be timed from the moment the green flag was dropped.

The men headed off toward the stands and London headed over to her truck which was already parked behind the starting blocks. She climbed aboard, put on her goggles and started the engine. She checked all the gauges, peddles and gears. Her white knuckles gripped the steering wheel as she waited, trying to breath easy and psych herself up for some fun and skill challenge.

The flag dropped, London mildly pushed the accelerator and she was off. She spent the first lap getting used to the truck. She wanted to get used to the peddles and the stick shift. She was curious how it would handle. She even checked the brakes, knowing that she didn't plan on using them until the finish. The second lap she focused on the course and its jumps, water holes, hairpin curves and the orange obstacle barrels. During the third time around she focused on the flow of the track and the dirt floor, so by the fourth lap she was starting to pick up speed and push the engine as far as necessary for her to get the idea of just how much power her truck was hauling. During the fifth and final trial lap she tried to combine all that she had just absorbed. In her mind she heard all the advice that had been given by the Greeters: 'Be true to yourself, trust truth and goodness, and to try to find the most pleasure out of everything you do.'

As she rounded the track and approached the starting line she heard a loud buzzer, saw the green flag drop and told herself this was it and that she'd better do her best and make the most out of the next ten laps.

The first nine times around were fun, fast and flawless. Only one more lap to go, the thought made London choke and get distracted. She started to doubt herself and as then tenth and final lap began, she down shifted to get control of her truck (and herself). But, as she did, she felt the fingernail on her pinky finger of her right hand hit the passenger seat and snap. In a split second she missed a gear, faltered and threw off her own rhythm. A sickened London looked down at her broken nail and thought 'Now you've done it, no mercy for a self inflicted injury, what were you thinking? Monsters trucks? You're no driver and now you are going to fail because you made a bad choice to begin with... Monster trucks? Please...Darn it...Just keep your focus and finish this mess or you may never get home.'

Just as she was looking back up at the course she hit a small puddle, slid to the right and heard a strange guzzle sound come from underneath the hood. Focusing her attention on the new noise instead of the off-road track she ran right into a bright orange obstacle barrel. A loud buzzer rang and the truck turned off immediately by itself. The control tower above had activated the automatic kill switch.

London sat there a moment, took off her helmet and climbed down out of the truck. She expected to see Nathan and Thaniel, but what she didn't expect to see were all four of her grandparents sitting with the Greeters. She wanted to run up and tell them how much that she had missed them and that she was sorry that she had done so poorly. It was her Mamaw Bertie that stood up and came around the grandstand gates to unite with London on the dirt floor.

Bertie took London's arm and said, "Don't feel so bad, you know that I have always told you that everything happens for a reason."

London started to protest and rationalize such a blunder over a broken nail, but she was hushed by her Mamaw. Walking towards the pits Bertie began to tell London a secret, "Sssshhhh. Listen carefully London. Your Papaw Sam has been talking to that fellow Thaniel. Seems he is not just a grease monkey. His Earth name was Thane. It means 'higher privilege.' Anyways, they have been working together along with your other grandparents Faye and Bill to get an appointment with Robbie to plead on your behalf. It worked. It has already taken place and Thaniel, Thane, himself, traveled to Earth and researched your scrambled data from that end. The best we can tell is that you WERE taken too early and you should not be here yet. What Robbie said was that they didn't want London England from Alice, Texas. They wanted Alice Texas from London, England. She isn't 37, she is 73...You're married to Jim Madrid from Chicago, and her Husband was 'Chicago' Jim from Madrid. And instead of a daughter Brandi, they had one son named Brandon... London, do you hear me?"

London, in shock stuttered, "So I was right all along? It wasn't my time, and now I have blown this one last trial?"

"Don't be so sure, London. That is still being worked out," eased Bertie.

"Do I get to go back? I love you Mamaw, thank you sooo much. It is sooo good to see you," gushed London.

Bertie continued, "We don't have the authority or the power to return you to Earth, butwe were able to set up the interview with Robbie for you. You are expected back on Upper-Anaheim to speak with him as soon as possible."

"That's better than nothing!" London tried to sound positive and up beat for all the gratitude she felt for their help, but she had been transported around too many times. "Are you coming with me?"

"No, I am sorry; we were actually moving on to orb-phase three when all of this happened, but we wanted to make sure you were OK, and we will be hoping the best for you. Trust truth that our love is complete. Now go get out of that jump suit, there will be a white robe in the pit-stop for you."

London did as she was told. Naturally, when she came out of the changing room, like so many of the planets before, she had already moved on to a different place. She wasn't in Mechanic Majestics anymore; it was Robbie's Interview Inn. She called out to him, but he didn't respond. She thought maybe he was testing another Returner so she sat down by the waterfall. When Robbie didn't appear for quite some time, she had a second thought that he might be in his personal resting place so she went behind the waterfall, and through the hidden door.

London yelled for him again, "Robbie, are you in here?"

She waited momentarily, but there was still no sign of him. She decided to lay down awhile and get some well needed rest. How ironic; this was the first time that she got the chance to nap since she had begun all of these adventures.

She didn't know how long she had been there or where Robbie had been, but she was beginning to be aware of a hand gently shaking her awake.

"London, London, London wake up."

"Huh?" she said, stirring, stretching and forcing her eyes to open.

"London, come on. Wake up."

"OK, do I get to go back to Earth?" pleaded London with the same question she had asked over and over again.

"WHAT?"

The voice was so clear and so loud that it made London snap awake. There, standing before her wasn't Robbie, Greeters, or her grandparents, but her own truelove, sweetheart, Jim Madrid.

She was still laying down with her eyes, nose and mouth wide open, and there he was right beside her, so close that he looked like a hovering angel.

He spoke, "Come on baby, it's time to go to bed. Find the remote so we can turn off the TV."

London sat straight up, looked at Jim and then at the screen. The announcer said, "That concludes our science fiction marathon… Coming up next, your local news." With one enormous sigh of relief, London jumped up to get the remote from the usual spot on the side table. The quick action and rapid movement made her dizzy and off balance. She was still groggy and still confused. Sitting back down was positively the right course of action to take.

This pause for the cause made her contemplate. She began massaging her temples to try to align her swimming thoughts. Was it only a dream? Or did she really get to return? All of her destinations seemed so real. The Soulotomy at the Interview Inn; Foodland Fanacity, Sports Sphere, Animal Eden, Amusemetropolis, Video Utopia, and Mechanic Majestics with it being her grandparents and Thane making everything work out. What about her other greeters and their special names Elle/

LaWeez (Elloise); Steph/Fanny (Stephanie); Vic/Tori (Victory); Alex/Xander (Alexander); Abby/Gail (Abigail); Zach/Kari (Zachery); and Nathan/Thaniel (Nathaniel) aka Thane. London thought to herself, 'I couldn't make all this up in one dream.' She had even seen all of her pets and favorite animal activist like Marty. And, she couldn't help but remember the explanation that she had received about Alice Texas in London England with similar scrambled information. She was 73 not 37. Her Husband was Chicago Jim from Madrid, not Jim Madrid from Chicago. And she had a son named Brandon. We have Brandi. She smiled at the thought of Beenie. This one image brought her back to reality.

It's all too unbelievable. It's impossible... It had to be a dream. But... As she climbed the stairs behind Jim, reaching for the banister, her attention was drawn towards her right hand, because there she noticed that the pinky fingernail was broken. She gasped and whispered to herself, "Oh, my heavens."

The End.